50
90
011

# THE CRIME OF COY BELL

## Sam Brown

Walker and Company
New York

First published in the United States of America in 1992
by Walker Publishing Company, Inc.

Published simultaneously in Canada by Thomas Allen & Son
Canada, Limited, Markham, Ontario

Library of Congress Cataloging-in-Publication Data
Brown, Sam, 1945–
The crime of Coy Bell/Sam Brown.
p.  cm.
ISBN 0-8027-4115-0
I. Title.
PS3552.R717C7   1992
813'.54—dc20      91-30222
CIP

Printed in the United States of America

2  4  6  8  10  9  7  5  3  1

# CONTENTS

# THE CRIME OF
# COY BELL

Also by Sam Brown

*The Trail to Honk Ballard's Bones*
*The Long Season*

# PROLOGUE

For some time Coy Bell was one of the most wanted, hated, and misunderstood men in the history of the West.

The story of Coy Bell is a portrait of heartache, bloodshed, and love. It could not have occurred in any other time or place than it did—a time and place where the will of a Winchester often, and many times by necessity, was stronger than the will of the Law . . .

# PART I

## A LITTLE SUNSHINE
## IN COY'S LIFE

# CHAPTER 1

Broad-shouldered and lanky, spurs jingling with each step, Coy Bell laid his saddle and saddle blankets in the dirt of the horse corrals of the VanHughes Ranch nine miles west of Decatur, Texas, in the year 1888. After a quick inspection of the eight head of horses in the corral, he shook out a big loop in his limber catch rope. His sharp blue eyes settled on a thin, high-withered brown, and a few seconds after that the rope settled over that same brown's neck, flicked expertly over his head with an easy hoolihand toss.

The brown snorted and pawed once at the rope, then let himself be led toward the saddle on the ground. Coy carefully bridled the brown and eased the saddle blankets and saddle onto the horse's back.

Coy Bell smiled as the horse humped his back underneath the saddle.

It was just another job on another cow outfit for Coy. He had hired on just that morning to go out with the wagon and work during spring branding. J.D. Davis, the outfit's wagon boss, had pointed out which horses in the remuda would be in Coy's string, then gone about his own business of being sure everything was ready to get the crew of cowboys out on the range the next day. Coy separated his string of horses from the rest of the remuda so he could top them all out. Most of them had not been ridden since the works had finished the fall before, and Coy knew some of them might have a few wrinkles in their backs that would need some ironing out.

Coy tightened his cinches on the brown, untracked him

by leading him forward a few steps, then turned him around. He reached up and pulled his hat down tightly on his head, shook the saddle a time or two, gathered the reins up short, and eased himself into the saddle seat, boots deep in oxbow stirrups.

The lanky brown looked back and snorted.

"Okay, Mister Son of a Bitch," Coy said softly as he pulled the horse's head around and tried to coax him into taking a step, "let's dance this set easy."

But instead of dancing easy, the horse squealed like a hog and blew up like a bundle of dynamite.

This wasn't a rodeo with cheering crowds and cash prizes and a kid with something to prove. This was a cow-outfit horse corral, and Coy Bell was a hurricane-deck veteran of twenty years. The only rule here was to stay aboard and the prize was that if you did, you wouldn't get your head stuck in the horse-corral dirt. Therefore, Coy Bell pulled leather and turned his toes out so his spurs could dig into horse-belly hide.

The brown weakened after only a few jumps and Coy felt he had him covered. But the brown was bucking blindly toward the saddlehouse.

"You goofy bastard!" Coy yelled just before they hit the saddlehouse wall head-on.

The brown bounced off the wall, went to his knees in a cloud of dust, then hurled himself, and Coy, into the wall again, this time sideways.

The wall buckled, the roof above it sagged, and horse and rider went to the ground. The horse flounced twice, twitched once, then lay still. Coy scrambled out of the way, tried to get up, but fell beside the horse, clutching his left leg.

As the corral dust settled back gently to earth Coy knew the brown was dead, probably of a broken neck.

J.D. Davis came into the corral, walked over to where horse and cowboy were lying in the dirt, kicked the horse in the butt with a boot toe, spat tobacco juice in the dust, and said, "Looks like you've killed a pretty good horse, Bell."

Coy tried not to let the pain he was feeling in his leg show on his face. "Yeah," he said, "he was just the kind of son of a bitch every outfit needs."

"Doc Blanchard is coming out today to check Mister VanHughes," said J.D. "Maybe you'd better have him look at your leg while he's here."

"Hope it won't put anybody out," Coy said dryly.

Dr. Blanchard pronounced a bone in Coy's left leg to be broken and proceeded to twist and pull on it until he had it splinted like he wanted.

"Gosh, Doc," Coy complained, "I think runnin' into the saddlehouse was easier on me than you were."

As soon as Dr. Blanchard left the bunkhouse, J.D. and Walter Davis entered. Coy forced a grin on his sun-browned face, thinking that surely the pair was bringing what he felt he had coming from the outfit—a little sympathy and a lot of whiskey.

This was the first time Coy had seen Walter Davis, but he knew who he was, just like he knew, from talking to other cowboys, that Walter was old Leonard VanHughes's son-in-law. The ranch was known as the VanHughes Ranch by nearly everybody, but it was also widely known that it was now Walter Davis who was calling the shots and making the managerial decisions.

Walter Davis was a man crowding fifty, with a full, graying red beard and gray eyes. He was thickset, stood straight as a poker, and looked serious as a revival preacher. But it was his younger brother J.D. who now did the talking—and the distributing of ranch sympathy.

"Bell," J.D. said, "you won't be much use to us now. Walter says you can stay here in the bunkhouse for a while, but in a couple of days you'll have to start helping the caretaker with his work. We're not goin' to pay you, though—we figure boarding you will be more than adequate compensation. If you don't help old Jewel, you don't stay. We're not going to have some freeloading cowboy staying here and not working—especially not after he's just killed one of our best horses.

"Me and Walter will be out with the wagon for the next couple of months, but one of us will be in from time to time and we'll know whether you're working or not, so don't try to take advantage of our generosity. You don't work, and we've told Jewel to take you right back to Decatur and dump you out."

All the while J.D. was talking, Coy had been working on his own speech in which he planned to instruct Walter and brother J.D. on just what exactly they could do with their "generosity." But by the time Coy could get a word in, the Davises were walking back to the big house on the hill, so he had to be content with unloading his entire speech to an empty bunkhouse.

Or at least Coy thought the bunkhouse was empty, except for himself. He didn't know until after he had finished his closing remarks and heard old Pete Jewel softly laughing that he had had an audience after all.

Coy rolled over, looked at Pete Jewel's smiling black face, and said, "And you can go straight to hell, mister."

# CHAPTER 2

For all of his complaining for the next few days about his sour luck and what he thought was extreme suffering on his part, the break in Coy's leg was actually not a bad one. Even he had had worse. Just one of the bones below the left knee had been fractured, and it had been a clean break, the kind that heals quickly. Still, Coy thought with an inward smile, *if I don't give myself a little sympathy I sure as hell won't get any, not on this outfit.*

Old Pete Jewel followed his orders to a T and on the third morning following Coy's leg break, he carried all the shovels, axes, and hoes he could find into the bunkhouse for Coy to sharpen with a file.

"Good gawdamighty, Jewel," Coy said. "I didn't know there was that many damn implements in the whole world."

That afternoon Jewel brought in a crutch he had made and handed it to Coy.

"I guess," Coy said, "this means you're not going to carry my meals over from the cookhouse anymore, don't it?"

"It do, Mistuh Bell," Jewel said with a nod.

"Oh, goddammit, Jewel," Coy chided, "quit callin' me Mister Bell!"

"Yessuh, Mistuh Coy."

Coy laughed and shook his head. "Something else, Jewel—I haven't touched a single ax, shovel, or hoe once, and I'm not going to. If I did sharpen them, my heart wouldn't be in it and I would only do a half-good job. I

7

figure in a case like that, no job at all is better than a half-good one."

Now Jewel laughed. "At least you is honest, Mistuh Coy, and I admires that in a man."

"Well, since you aren't going to bring my grub to me anymore, I think I'll use this crutch and start hobbling over to the cookhouse and see what the cook has stirred up."

As Jewel and Coy were slowly coming back toward the bunkhouse from the cookhouse, Coy stopped to rest a few moments and as he did so he looked around the headquarters complex and said, "This is *some* fancy place, isn't it. Reminds me of a southern plantation."

What Coy was specifically referring to was the big, white house on the rise of ground to the north. Two big red barns, saddlehouse, bunkhouse, cookhouse, wagon shed, hay shed, the big layout of horse and cattle corrals—none of these looked out of place on a Texas cow outfit.

But that big, white, two-story house on the rise to the north, shaded by huge willow trees, with its tall white pillars and screened-in porches upstairs and down, and the curving rock steps in the green yard leading up to it from the white picket fence around it, it looked just like pictures he had seen taken in Georgia or Alabama.

"The VanHugheses is plantation folk," Jewel said. "Mistuh Leonard come here afta the war and 'stablished this cow ranch. I come with 'im . . . but I come as a freedom-found man. I can leave any time I takes the notion."

"Reckon you'll ever take that notion, Jewel?"

"Ain't likely, not as long as Mistuh Leonard or Miss Laurel is alive. They've been—That's them comin' out onto the top porch now," Jewel said, looking at the house. "Miss Laurel is bringin' Mistuh Leonard out to get a little sun. He's in a wheelchair for three years now, and he shore has got crotchety, but Miss Laurel, she takes good care o' him.' "

The remainder of that week passed, and Coy could tell that his leg was going to heal faster than he had thought it might. It was still painful, especially at night, but it seemed to him that he could actually feel the broken bone knitting itself together. In no more than ten days, two weeks tops, he told himself, he should be able to ride—but not *for* the VanHughes outfit. He planned to ride *away* from them as soon as he could.

Jewel did a lot of piddling work in the coming days, everything from mending a broken spoke on a hay wagon to building a new saddle rack in the saddlehouse and trying to straighten out the wall that had cracked and bowed when Coy and the brown horse plowed into it.

Coy did not like to think he'd swallowed his cowboy pride and gone to work—he preferred to say he got bored sitting around the bunkhouse alone and decided helping old Jewel was about the only way he could relieve that boredom. Mostly, what he did was hand Jewel a nail now and then, or hold a pair of pliers for him.

Coy never saw J.D. Davis come in at all, but Walter Davis came in once during that first week, stayed a couple of hours, and left again before sundown. Coy heard him ask Jewel if he was getting any work out of "that cowboy."

Early Monday morning of the first day of Coy's second week at the ranch, right after breakfast at the cookhouse, Jewel announced that it was time to start digging a ditch. Coy grinned and announced, in return, that it was time he was drifting, broken leg or no.

"Won't be much burden on you to help me," Jewel said, with a tone of good-natured sarcasm and a slight plea in his voice. "I'll swing the pick and do most o' the shovelin'. All you got to do is help me clean the dirt out o' the bottom of the ditch with a nice short-handled shovel you can use while you lay on the ground."

Coy considered the proposition a moment, grinned, and said, "One drop of sweat and I'm rattlin' my hocks outa here, Jewel."

But Coy *did* sweat. Not so much from hard labor but from the humid Texas May morning. It was one of those days like north Texas can have when you can sweat doing nothing more than sitting in the shade. So he sweated, but he did not rattle his hocks out of there like he had promised in the cookhouse, not then anyway. Had he kept that good-natured promise he would never have met Laurel May Davis. Had he never met Laurel May Davis he could have ridden out much the uncomplicated and simple man he had been when he rode in.

It was about midmorning when the screen door on the downstairs porch opened and slammed shut. Coy looked up from the bottom of the ditch to see Mrs. Walter Davis coming down the rock steps toward him and Jewel. She carried a tray and was wearing a light blue dress that was made of something soft and slick that sure wasn't calico or gingham, the only two women's fabrics Coy recognized on sight, excluding barroom satin, of course.

Her blonde hair was pulled back from her face and tied with a blue ribbon.

"I thought you two looked like you could use some lemonade, Jewel," she said as she stopped at the yard gate about ten feet from where Coy was lying on the ground on his belly looking up at her.

"Yessum, Miss Laurel," Jewel said as he dropped his shovel. "That's some thoughtful of you."

With his splinted leg, Coy got up awkwardly from his stomach to his feet. When he was finally standing upright and had his crutch under his left arm, he saw that both Jewel and Mrs. Davis were watching him. "Sort of do it like an old cow, don't I," he jested, removing his hat to wipe the sweat off his forehead with a shirt sleeve.

"Does it hurt much, Mister—?" Laurel May Davis asked.

Putting his hat back on his head and reaching for his glass of lemonade from the tray, Coy said, "Coy Bell . . . and yes, ma'am, it hurts something terrible. I haven't experienced anything like it in years. Don't know if I'll *ever* get over it, either."

"You mean to say you think you may be permanently crippled?" she inquired.

"Most likely," Coy said, and then took a long drink of lemonade.

"Maybe Jewel should take you to town to see Doctor Blanchard again . . . Maybe he needs to have another look at that leg."

Coy lowered the glass. "The leg's doin' fine, ma'am."

"But you said . . ."

Coy Bell grinned, showing even white teeth. "I was talking about my wounded pride and the permanent damage to my reputation if word should ever get out to certain cow camps that I've been diggin' in the dirt like a gopher."

Jewel grinned, shook his head, and put his empty glass back on Mrs. Davis's tray.

"Thank you, ma'am," Coy said as he, too, put his glass on the tray.

"You're welcome, gentlemen," Laurel May said cheerfully as she turned to go back up the rock steps to the big house. But she stopped short, turned back, and said, "And don't worry, Mister Bell, your secret is safe with me— besides that, you're doing such a *wonderful* job!"

"Yes, ma'am," Coy replied, leaning on his crutch. "Probably the world's champion dirt-scoopin' cowboy—at least from the belly position."

# CHAPTER 3

The next day Jewel and Coy were back at work on the ditch. It nearly broke Coy's heart when Jewel told him the ditch had to be about twice as wide, twice as long, and twice as deep as it already was. Coy didn't say much as he got down on his belly with his short-handled shovel, mumbling to himself.

Coy could have left, but the fact was he wasn't hurting himself any. Besides, it was quiet and peaceful around the place with all the other hands gone, he and Jewel had a good time ribbing each other, and the food the Mexican cook put on the table at the cookhouse was better than cold beans and tomatoes. So Coy stayed because it made more sense to do that than to leave with a broken leg.

About midmorning a fringe-topped surrey arrived at the ranch, carrying three high-headed ladies. As they passed through the yard gate, Coy rolled over, tipped his hat to them and said, "Good mornin'." Only one of them had the decency to respond at all, and hers was no more than a grunt, the kind Coy had heard lazy old horses make when kicked in the ribs.

Mrs. Davis met them at the porch door with her own cheery hello. She got a little more out of the trio in the way of response than Coy had, as one of them—Coy figured the grunter of the bunch—said, "Laurel May, who in the world is that scruffy-looking man with the splint on his leg?"

Coy knew that kindly, God-fearing lady meant her remark to be nothing more than constructive criticism, and that's the way he took it—he shaved at noon for the first time since he'd been at the ranch, over a week.

Later in the day Laurel May Davis came down the steps, carrying refreshments. She was wearing a white dress with lace at the collar and sleeves and two rows of buttons down the front. Her hair was put up in a bun at the back of her head. She was no less beautiful than she had been the day before. Her eyes were just as blue, her eyebrows and lashes just as thick, her nose and soft-looking lips just as delicate, her jaw and chin just as refined, and her figure below just as graceful and womanly as a man could want to admire.

"Maggie made some cookies for the ladies from the church," she said as she arrived at the picket gate, "and I set some aside for you two."

"That's some thoughtful of you, Miss Laurel," Jewel said as he reached for his share.

"Yes, ma'am," Coy agreed, reaching for his lemonade and a couple of cookies from the tray, "it sure is. Much obliged . . . Maggie must have been one of the three ladies who came in the surrey."

"Oh, no," Laurel May said. "Maggie is the housekeeper and cook."

Coy nodded and grinned, but didn't say anything, glancing toward the big white house and thinking not about plantations and such, but about castles and servants and knights and kings. Coy guessed Walter Davis was her knight. Or was he the king? But if he *was* the king, what was old Leonard VanHughes? Coy was playfully trying to sort that out in his mind and get everybody assigned to their proper roles in the fairy tale, when a gruff voice from an upstairs window yelled, "Black Jewel! Black Jewel! Come up here!"

Coy laughed inside. Seeing how fast the old man moved, Coy thought Jewel must have been summoned by the king himself.

"You all are really doing well with the ditch, Mister Bell."

"Yes, ma'am," Coy said. "Will the crocodiles be gettin' here pretty soon?"

"Wha . . . what?" she asked.

"Crocodiles," Coy said again. "Jewel never has told me what the ditch is for, but adding everything up I figure it must be a moat for this castle."

"Mister Bell . . ."

Coy was afraid she was going to take offense at what he had said, but then she smiled and dropped her head in laughter. She came through the picket gate to Coy's side of the fence and stood beside him above the ditch and looked down at it.

"Roses," she said.

Now it was Coy's turn to look puzzled and say, "What?"

"Roses," she said again. "There will be rosebushes planted in this ditch. All along this side of the fence."

"Rosebushes," Coy said, sort of disappointed. "I'm helping dig a ditch to plant a bunch of flowers in . . . I wish it *had* been a moat."

She laughed a little again and then said, "But they will be so pretty here in front of the fence. And *something* needs to be growing here besides goatheads."

Coy tilted his head back and bit his lip in thought. "How does that line go about roses . . . 'Roses are planted where thorns grow and on the barren heath sing the honey bees.' That's it! Now you'll have to have some honey bees and a barren heath—whatever a barren heath is!"

Laurel had a look of utter and complete disbelief on her face. "My God . . . *you*? You can quote from 'The Marriage of Heaven and Hell'?"

"Not sure what it was called. I know it was written by a man named Blake—because that's what I named my bay horse, and I got the name from this book I read that someone left in a line camp where I spent last winter. He's a good one too—the bay horse, I mean."

Laurel May laid her hand for a second on Coy's forearm

as she laughed. Then she removed the hand, straightened up, and said, "You are a remarkable man, Mister Bell."

"Laurel May! Laurel May! Come here!" It was the same gruff voice that had summoned Jewel just minutes earlier, coming from the same upstairs window.

"Father needs me," she said. "I'd better go."

From then on Laurel May brought refreshments out twice a day. Sometimes after Jewel had picked up his pick or shovel and returned to work, she and Coy would sit in the shade of the nearby willow tree and talk for a few minutes—and usually have a laugh or two—before she went back into the house.

One morning when she came down the stone steps in the yard with her tray, Coy stood up—by then the splint had been taken off and he could get to his feet without difficulty—and said, "Good mornin', Sunshine."

"Who?" she said.

"Sunshine," Coy said again, smiling. He didn't really know why he said it—it just came to him as he saw her walking down those stone steps with her golden hair catching the morning sun, like cottonwood leaves do after an early-morning shower. She seemed to make the whole day a little brighter, like sunshine itself.

Suddenly Coy looked over Laurel's shoulder and saw the plump form of Maggie standing on the porch, watching them. Laurel had told him the day before, laughingly, that her cook and housekeeper had informed her that she was being far too informal with the hired help of late—it didn't look proper. They both laughed when Coy told her that he really wasn't hired help since he wasn't drawing any wages. But still, when he saw Maggie standing on the porch and probably within hearing range, he cleared his throat and said louder, but with a little grin, "Good morning . . . Mrs. Davis."

They had, in just a few days, become good friends. How

could a cowboy and a lady like Laurel May Davis be good friends? Coy wasn't sure. They seemed as different as night and day, but still they never lacked for anything to talk about, and the talk came easy for them.

The person Coy could not understand was Walter Davis. During the month since Coy had broken his leg, Walter Davis had not spent three nights in his own bed—with Laurel May. Sure, Coy knew the outfit's wagon was out and they were busy branding. But Coy also knew Walter had a wagon boss—brother J.D.—who was supposed to be running that part of the operation. Coy thought maybe Walter was one of those men who didn't think a brand would peel unless he was there to smell the branding smoke. But still, Coy couldn't understand any man leaving a woman like Laurel May alone as many nights as Walter did.

Late one afternoon as he saw Walter leaving the house to return to the wagon where he would sleep on the ground, Coy caught himself thinking it would take a good team of draft horses to pull himself away from that house with night coming on so close.

Sometime that night, not long after Coy had first gone to sleep, the sound of a horse's squeal awakened him. He slipped on his clothes and walked to the corrals to make sure some long-toothed VanHughes horse wasn't skinning up his little bay.

He looked through the boards of the corral and saw that it was two ranch horses having a little row and that his bay was on the other side of the pen minding his own business.

Coy stood there a few minutes watching the horses, and before long his bay and a ranch horse came over to the side of the corral where he was. Coy reached a hand out and let them smell it.

"You like horses, don't you?"

Coy turned around and behind him, with a shawl around her shoulders, was Laurel May. He leaned against the fence, laughed a little, and said, "Most of 'em, which is a pretty good thing considering the work I do. Horses are like people, though—some of them you can't like no matter how hard you try . . . I didn't know anyone else was out here."

She shrugged her shoulders and said, "I couldn't sleep, so I thought I'd take a walk . . . it's so quiet and peaceful out here."

"Not much can compare to a Texas spring night," Coy said. She walked to the corral and put her own hand through the fence. Coy's bay stretched out his neck and sniffed it. She scratched the horse on the muzzle and he took a step forward. Then she tried to pet him between the eyes and he wheeled away and left.

"Most horses don't like to be rubbed between the eyes," Coy told her, "because they can't see for sure what your hand is doing and it makes 'em nervous."

They stood there, leaning on the fence and looking into the moonlit corral for a while without saying anything. An owl in the cottonwoods to the east hooted a time or two, and two horses on the other side of the corral scratched each other's withers.

"This is sure a pretty place you folks have here," Coy said.

"Where is your home, Coy?" she asked.

Coy laughed a little and said, "A man like me's home is where he unrolls his bed."

She turned around and put her elbows on a corral board, looked at him, and said, "And what kind of a man is 'a man like me'?"

"Oh, I'm sure you've heard of us . . . drifters . . . irresponsible . . . ne'er-do-wells . . . rolling stones . . . cowboys." Coy turned around to face her and shrugged.

"And where will you go when you leave here?" she asked.

Coy shrugged again. "Haven't really thought about it."

Another short silence, then she said, "I envy you in a

way—just being able to saddle up and leave anytime you want and go to someplace new."

Coy had to laugh at that. "That's something new—a rich Texas lady saying she envies a cowboy whose total fortune's probably not worth the dress she's wearin' . . . a queen in a castle."

"A queen?" she said with a little laugh. Then there was a long silence before she said, "Yes, Coy . . . but it's a lonely castle."

Coy looked at her and saw her for the first time—really saw her. He saw the beauty, yes—but also the loneliness— in her eyes. Coy *felt* her loneliness, just like he suddenly felt his own, and felt it strong. He wasn't expecting it— what he saw, what he felt—and it hit him with a jolt.

Suddenly Laurel May pulled the shawl up higher on her shoulders, turned toward her house, and said, "Good night" without looking back.

The next day she did not bring any lemonade or cookies out to Coy and Jewel. But the day after that she did, and that was the day they planted the bushes in the ditch they had been digging. Laurel May and Coy talked and laughed that day like they had before, but at times—when their eyes met—it was not like the other days, it was like that night in the moonlight by the corral, only stronger . . . and lonelier.

# CHAPTER 4

Coy did not see Laurel May for the next two days, except late in the afternoons when she would be standing out on the upstairs porch alone. But he could not get her out of his mind no matter how hard he tried or what he did. He told himself what a fool he was—a grown man, a drifting cowboy with a rich married lady on his mind. True, at times he thought about being in bed with her, but he could understand and account for that, that's how most men thought about women.

But he really enjoyed just being with her and talking to her, and that was something strange for him, something he could not fully understand or account for. And she was a married woman! He had *never* had a married woman on his mind. Married! He did not take marriage vows lightly, nor the commandment to not covet another man's wife.

No matter what he did or how much he chastised himself, his mind wouldn't let go. He couldn't sleep at night, but instead would lay on his bunk and look up into the darkness. Every time he closed his eyes he would see her face and the loneliness in her eyes—and every time he saw her loneliness, he felt his own.

One night after dark, when he should have been asleep for at least an hour, he said to Jewel, "How'd it happen, Jewel?" Jewel was sound asleep and didn't hear him, so he threw a boot toward Jewel's bunk and said it again, only louder, "Jewel! How in the hell did it happen?!"

Jewel stirred on his cot and finally said, "Glory be, Mistuh Coy, what is you talkin' about, and why ain't you asleep?"

19

"Laurel May and Walter," Coy said. "How did it happen?"

After a silence, Jewel said, "Mistuh Leonard . . . that's how it happened."

"Her father?"

"The VanHugheses and the Davises was both old-South families. When Mistuh Leonard got sick and crippled he couldn't run the ranch no more. Mistuh Walter was a family friend—and he has a good head on his shoulders, at least accordin' to Mistuh Leonard. So . . . ."

"So you mean old Leonard VanHughes picked Walter Davis out himself—he picked a man twenty-five years older than Laurel May to be her husband—a man she didn't love—just because he had the right blood and a good business head? Didn't she have *any* say-so in the matter?"

"I s'pose she could've said no, but if she had, it would've been the first time in her life she say that word to Mistuh Leonard. She'd 'bout do anything he wanted."

"Since she wasn't the son old Leonard always wanted, huh, she made up for it by lettin' him pick her husband for her? Good god! The old bastard!"

"What's done is done, Mistuh Coy. Mistuh Davis is a fair man an' he's done well for the ranch—him and Mistuh Leonard gets on good together."

"Well, I'll bet that's a comfort to Laurel May!" Coy said.

"Leave it be, Mistuh Coy . . . Leave it be."

Two more days passed without Coy and Laurel May seeing each other. She did not even come out on the upstairs porch late in the afternoons. She was still as strong on his mind as ever, but it suddenly hit Coy that he had to leave. His leg was well enough for him to ride, and he knew it was the only thing for him to do. He would get away from the VanHughes Ranch, go somewhere and hire on with some good cow outfit somewhere else, and forget about her. But could he leave without seeing her again?

He never really got a chance to find out, because the very next morning while he was feeding the horses Maggie yelled for him and Jewel to come up to the house—"Quick!"

When they got to the front door of the house, Laurel May met them there in a panic. "Daddy's had another attack, Jewel!" she said.

"Mistuh Coy," Jewel said, "go hitch a team to the wagon an' bring 'er up to the gate! I'll go see 'bout Mistuh Leonard!"

Coy hitched the team as quickly as possible, pulled the wagon close to the yard gate, then went inside the house to see old Leonard VanHughes lying on the couch in the parlor. "Help me carry him to the wagon!" Jewel said. While the men were doing that, Laurel May and Maggie made a pallet out of blankets in the wagon bed.

The old man was limp and clammy as they started out the door with him, and Coy thought he might die at any time, but by the time they were laying him on the pallet in the wagon bed he was beginning to mumble and to sling his arms around like a thrashing machine.

Coy was told to grab the lines and head out for Decatur, while Laurel May and Jewel sat beside Leonard and tried to hold him down, as, by then, he was cussing all and making it plain that he was not interested in seeing anything outside of his room.

They made the nine miles to Decatur as fast as was possible without killing the horses. By the time they got there, Coy was thinking the old man needed a club over the head worse than he needed any doctoring. But it was a doctoring Laurel May was determined he would have, so of course that's what he got.

After Dr. Blanchard checked him over from one end to the other in his office, he took off his glasses and looked at Laurel May. "It seems like he's just had another one of those crazy spells like he's had off and on for the last couple of years. I can't say what causes them or when he'll have another one, but he seems to be okay now. Just to be safe though, Laurel May, I think it would be best if he stayed here—at least until tomorrow."

"Well, I'll be goddamned if I'm stayin' *here*," old Leonard VanHughes said. "Jewel, go over to the Cattlemen's Hotel and get us a room!"

Laurel May looked at Dr. Blanchard. "He'd probably be just as well off at the hotel as here, Laurel May," the doctor said. "I won't be more than a minute or two away—not that I think he will need me."

"Fine," Laurel May said. "I'll stay too."

"You will not!" Leonard said. "You'll go back to the ranch where you belong." He looked at Coy. "This feller will take you . . . You're not going to stay at a hotel that's full of whiskey drinkin' and loose women."

Dr. Blanchard looked at Laurel May and said, "I really don't think there's any need for you to stay. Why don't you go on home like Leonard said—he can probably go back tomorrow himself."

Laurel May sat up on the wagon seat with Coy, not close, and except for the rattle of wagon and harness, they rode in silence for the first two miles, each avoiding looking at the other, eyes cast straight ahead on the road.

Finally Coy said, "Do you think he'll be okay?"

"I think so," Laurel May said. "He's had these attacks before, and when they're over with he seems to be fine. It still scares me every time he has one, though."

That broke the silence, and they talked and laughed as the horses plodded along in a walk with their heads down and the wagon wheels slowly ground out the miles.

The wagon road ran parallel to the Trinity River and about a half mile north of it. Two small creeks, about three miles apart, headed in the hills to the north and fed into the Trinity. Both of those small creeks had to be crossed on any trip to or from town, but they were gravel-bottomed and seldom offered any trouble. Many times the creeks would be dry, but the spring had been wet and they both had a little stream of clear, cool water in them now.

The horses had gotten pretty hot during the fast trip into town, so when they got to the easternmost creek Coy pulled the team to a stop and let them lower their heads and take on a fill of water. Coy decided he needed a drink himself, so he got out of the wagon and took on his own fill. Then Laurel May decided she would do the same.

After drinking their fill they sat on the creek bank in the grass. It was a pretty spring afternoon and the world seemed to be turning slowly. If there was a need to hurry now, neither of them could see it.

"Is it true, what Jewel told me about your old daddy picking Walter to be your husband?" Coy asked.

Laurel May was silent for a few moments, then said, "You're one person I don't think I could ever lie to, Coy . . . Yes, it *is* true—but I had known Walter for a long time, and I gave my approval. I wasn't forced into it."

"Good god, Sunshine, why'd you ever do it? Why did you marry a man you don't love?"

"I've never said that I don't love Walter. I just said he was the man Daddy thought I should marry . . . What about you?" she said, changing the subject. "Do you think you'll ever be married?"

Coy laughed out loud. "Sunshine," he said, "I'm thirty-two years old and haven't stayed in the same place more than a few months in fifteen years. The only thing I've got to my name is that bay horse at the ranch, a worn-out saddle, a bedroll, and a few clothes. I don't know how to do anything but punch cows for thirty dollars a month . . . Now, do *you* think I'll ever be married?"

"I think you have a lot to offer if you should ever decide to ask someone," Laurel May said.

"Well, in that case which do you think I should offer

first, the worn-out saddle or the bedroll—because *nobody's* gettin' that bay horse."

Laurel May lay in the grass, looked up at the tree leaves over them, and laughed.

Then they heard thunder for the first time. It wasn't a far-off low rumble, either, but close and loud enough to make them sit up at once. While they had been tarrying and talking and not paying attention, thunderclouds had been brewing and building in the northwest. It was hard for Coy to believe that he hadn't noticed them before, but he hadn't.

Coy stood up, looked at the dark bottoms of the clouds and their tall cottony tops, and said, "We'd better get to rattlin' that wagon."

Thunder rolled again as they started on down the road, and by the time they had covered another mile it began to get dark. The green hills in the northwest couldn't be seen now because of the rain falling on them.

"Looks like we're liable to get wet before we get to the ranch," Coy said, warning her and slapping the horses' butts with the heavy lines.

By the time they were halfway to the west creek they felt the first drops of rain. The drops were far apart but so big they could be heard when they hit.

Then a cold wind started blowing out of the cloud. "Feels like it could be coming off hail," Coy said. Thunder clapped almost overhead then, loud enough to frighten the horses. The air felt heavy and smelled wet.

The heavy rain hit them just as they started up the long slope that topped out above the west creek.

"We're going to get a soakin'," Coy told Laurel May, "but once we get across this next creek we should be able to make it to the ranch okay."

Coy ran the horses to the top of the slope, but pulled them to a quick stop when he saw the creek below them.

"Look down yonder," Coy said above the wind and rain,

"we're not fixin' to cross that for a while." The little creek that had been running a narrow stream of clear water was now full of brown, churning water that was higher in the middle than it was on either side, and it was already lapping out of the creek's banks and running through the green grass in the pasture.

Lightning sizzled and struck the hilltop next to the one they were on, making one of the horses rear up. "We'd better get off this hilltop!" Coy shouted.

When they got back to the foot of the slope the first small hailstones began to fall. "We'd better get underneath the wagon!" Coy told her.

Laurel May leaned into him and yelled, "There's an old abandoned homestead in those trees!" She was pointing to a little grove of cottonwoods up the draw about a half mile from where they were. Coy nodded, wheeled the team around to face them into the rain and hail, and took off toward the trees with the horses holding their heads low and shaking them.

"Better hold on," Coy said, "this may get rough!"

# CHAPTER 5

The homestead in the cottonwoods was nothing more than a collapsed adobe barn and a one-room adobe house that looked as if it could collapse any time. But it still had a roof, of sorts, and four walls.

Coy tied the horses' lines to a wagon wheel with their butts to the storm and helped Laurel May down, grabbing from underneath the seat the blankets that had made Leonard VanHughes's pallet.

Coy had to kick the door to get inside the house. The leather strips serving as door hinges broke and the door fell into the room, into a puddle of water on the dirt floor.

Inside it was dark and smelled musty, but the walls stopped the wind and the ceiling held back at least the greater part of the rain.

Although it was by now late in the afternoon it wasn't yet dark, not even with the storm, and in a few seconds their eyes adjusted to what light there was inside the adobe.

There was a small table with one broken leg, a broken hide-bottomed chair and a handmade cupboard still somehow hanging, at an angle, beside the rock fireplace on the north wall.

Coy stepped across a puddle of water and walked to a hole in the south wall where a window had been at one time. The rain, driven by the hard north wind, scarcely came in the window. Coy looked outside and said, "this isn't much, but it sure beats sittin' out there on a wagon seat."

Laurel May laughed.

"What's so funny?" Coy asked, holding his head back so he could see underneath his water-soaked and collapsed hat brim.

"You," she said.

He took off the hat, shook the water out of it, and tossed it into a dry corner.

"You look like you've just been baptized yourself," Coy said, seeing her wet clothes and the blonde hair that was plastered against her face. Then he saw that she was shivering.

"This is the driest thing we've got between us," he said, tossing her one of the blankets. "What do you reckon the chances are of there bein' any matches in this old thing?" he said as he walked across the room to the cupboard beside the fireplace.

"About like filling an inside flush," Laurel May said.

Coy laughed as he reached for the cupboard door.

"What's so funny?" she said. "Didn't you know that women know something about gambling?"

"Guess I didn't," Coy admitted, laughing harder, having a picture flash across his mind of Sunshine sitting at a table with a bunch of cigar-smoking, tobacco-chewing cowboys, trying to fill an inside flush. He carefully opened the cupboard door. Then, "Well, I'll be jiggered . . . There *are* some matches here—four of 'em and probably as old as I am."

"Looks like I just filled my inside flush then, doesn't it, Mister Smarty!"

Coy laughed again. "It sure does, Sunshine—and you win the hand, too. It's hard to beat one of those inside flushes, let me tell you!"

Coy broke up the table and chair and used his pocket knife to shave off some kindling. The first three matches never even sparked when he dragged them across a rock on the fireplace. He picked up the fourth one, and just before scraping it against the rock he looked up at Laurel

May, who stood beside him with the blanket around her shoulders, and said, "This may be about as hard as filling another inside flush." Then he dragged the match across the rock and watched it as it spluttered into flame, weak, but strong enough to light the kindling.

In a few minutes the fire had taken hold of the pieces of broken furniture. Laurel May stood in front of it, leaned forward, shook out her hair, dried it with one of the blankets, then let the fire finish drying it until it was soft as silk and gold as the rising sun. When she turned to face Coy, with the fire dancing off her hair and in her blue eyes, there was nothing he could do but stand and stare at her.

Outside there was total darkness by now, except for lightning flashes; and there was thunder, rain, hail, and a howling wind. But inside . . . inside was a warm fire, a flickering light . . .

"Sunshine," Coy whispered, moving to her and touching her soft cheek, feeling her warm breath on his hand.

"Coy . . . please," she whispered, looking up at him and then turning away and taking a step closer to the fire. "It's wrong, Coy."

"Yes," Coy said softly, "it is . . . but can you tell me how being married to a man you don't love is right?"

Coy stepped forward and stood close behind her, close enough to smell her hair. "And can you tell me how to stop lying awake at night thinking about you?"

Laurel May turned around slowly and looked up into his eyes. "If I knew that," she whispered, "then maybe I could sleep at night myself—instead of thinking about you down in the bunkhouse . . . Doesn't that sound terrible—coming from a respectable married woman. Or maybe I'm not so respectable after all."

Coy touched her soft cheek with his fingertips. "You're about the most respectable person I know . . . and one of the loneliest," he said, putting his arms around her and holding her body against his.

She didn't struggle against him, but laid her head on his chest. "We can't, Coy," she whispered. "Please . . . I'm asking you. It goes against everything I've ever been taught."

Still holding her tightly in his arms, smelling the fragrance of her hair, feeling the silkiness of it against his cheek, he said, "Sins of the flesh, huh?"

She nodded her head and whispered, "And the flesh is weak . . . but afterward . . . I couldn't look you in the face. Is that what you want?"

Coy was silent for several long seconds, then took her hand in his and said, "Then how about a dance? Isn't that a waltz the wind and rain are playing outside?"

Laurel May looked up and smiled happily. "Why, I believe it is, Mister Bell . . . Shall we? I think I *could* look you in the face after a waltz."

"Hello in there!" a man's voice yelled just before his heavy boots tromped onto the dry dirt floor of the adobe. "Wonder if you folks would mind sharin' this old place with the wife and I and our younguns. We're just travelin' through and got caught in the storm. Can't cross yonder creek and—"

"Come on in," Coy said, red-faced and smiling at Laurel May. "We got caught ourselves . . . in the storm, I mean."

The storm played itself out during the night and the morning star made its appearance brightly on the eastern horizon the next morning. They left the homestead at first light, found the creek fordable, and pulled into the ranch just after sunup.

As he politely helped Laurel May down from the wagon she said, "Coy, you have *got* to leave . . . you know that, don't you?"

"You won't be easy to forget," he said.

"But you will forget, just like I will—because we have no other choice."

"But we never got our dance," Coy said with a smile.

Laurel May smiled back. "No, we didn't, did we? But at least this morning we still have most of our self respect." Then tears suddenly glistened in her blue eyes. "Goodbye, Mister Bell," she said as she turned sharply around and walked to the big house on the hill.

# PART II

## LOOKING BACK

# CHAPTER 6

Three years and a few months later, in November of 1891, a cowboy sat alone on a bay horse atop a knoll overlooking the VanHughes Ranch headquarters. It was late in the day with the sun hanging low in the western sky. For several minutes the cowboy sat motionless in the saddle. Then suddenly he straightened in the saddle, touched a gentle spur to the bay's belly, and rode down toward the ranch buildings.

The place looked just like it had, thought Coy Bell as the little bay jig-trotted easily past the barn and stopped in front of the long bunkhouse.

"Hello, Pete Jewel!" Coy yelled. "You old black devil, you in there?"

Coy pushed his hat back, leaned forward in the saddle, rested his crossed forearms across the saddle horn, and waited. In a few seconds he yelled again, but no one answered or appeared behind the screen door of the bunkhouse.

Coy now looked nervously toward the big white house surrounded by willow trees on the rise of ground to the north. He pulled his hat back down and straightened in the saddle. Suddenly, he was not so sure about stopping to see old Pete Jewel and Laurel May. What would he say to Laurel May Davis? How would she react to him? If Walter were home, what would he think? But Coy only wanted to see her again, say hello to her as a friend, wish her the best of luck, and then ride on. That, he sincerely believed, was what he needed to do to put the matter to rest for once and for all. That done, he could leave it all on the trail behind him forever.

But now he was not so sure. Just being back at the ranch made him nervous. Still, he had come this close . . . he rode up the slope, stopped, and dismounted. He hobbled the bay in front of the rosebushes he and Laurel May had planted together. The rosebushes were dried up, dying even. The lawn was unkempt. Weeds were sprouting.

"Do something for you, mister?"

Coy looked up. An old man was standing in the doorway of the downstairs porch.

"Do something for you?" the old man repeated.

"Who're you?" Coy asked.

"More like, who in the hell are *you*?"

"Where's the people who live here?"

"You're lookin' at him."

"The Davises . . . old Leonard VanHughes . . . Laurel May Davis . . . everybody."

"Only me here. The new owners be movin' in shortly."

"The new owners? Where's the others?"

"Gone. Sold out, I reckon. I'm just a caretaker till the Brockmans get here."

"The Davises . . . Where'd they go?"

The old man shrugged. "Don't know. Might ask in town. I just work for the Brockmans, and they ain't moved in yet. Got cattle out on the range though—and cowboys too. You lookin' for work?"

"No," Coy finally said as he went back to the bay, pulled the hobbles off his forelegs, gathered his reins up, and mounted.

Just as Coy reined the bay around and started to ride away the old man yelled out, "Say . . . If you've been around here before . . . would you know a man named Bell?"

Coy stopped and turned in the saddle. "Maybe."

"Well, you might tell him that he's got a letter here. I

was told by somebody else who was told by I don't know who, that it was left here by the somebody who used to live here."

"A letter? I know Bell," said Coy. "I'll give it to him."

The old man disappeared into the house and came out shortly with an envelope, which he carried out to the picket gate and handed up to Coy.

Coy quickly inspected the sealed envelope, and the words COY BELL printed neatly across its front.

"You'll be sure he gets it?" the old man asked.

"He'll get it," Coy said as he put it into his shirt. He reined the bay around again to ride off. But before he did so, he looked over his shoulder and said to the old man standing in the picket gate, "Shame to let those pretty roses die, don't you think?"

The old man shrugged. "They're nothin' to me."

"I guess not," Coy said as he turned in the saddle and rode away.

Coy read the letter again, for the fourth time, and this time he read it by the light of a flickering camp fire several miles west of the old VanHughes Ranch:

*Dear Coy,*

*Part of me feels very foolish to be writing a letter to you—a letter you most probably will never see—but another part tells me it is something I need to do. So here I am, sitting at the kitchen table early in the morning, April 19, 1891, writing while everyone else is asleep—at least I hope they are asleep.*

*It has been almost three years since you left the ranch. How many times have I thought of you during those passing months and years? God only knows. I've tried to forget you, yet I have not. And, just as God knows how hard I have tried, He also knows the guilt I have suffered because I have not.*

*I thought that someday you would come back, you would call me your "Sunshine" again, and we would walk and talk and laugh*

*like we did before. Such foolish, sentimental—and immoral?—
thoughts from a married woman.*

*But you never came, which is for the best, I'm sure.*

*And now we are leaving—moving to somewhere in New Mexi-
co—for reasons I do not fully understand. We are packed and
ready. J.D. and the cowboys started with the cattle days ago. Daddy,
Jewel, Maggie, Walter, and I leave right after sunup. I will entrust
this letter with Jewel in hopes that he can find some way to leave it
where you will get it—if you ever do come back.*

*It is wrong for me to love you as I do, there is no doubt in my
heart about that. I should love Walter. God, how I have tried to
love him! I told myself that I would learn to love him after we were
married. But I have failed—I do not and cannot love him.*

*I have failed to be the wife I should have been to Walter, and
now I feel God has failed me, which I suppose is my just punishment. Daddy is all but blind now and his hearing is failing. Walter
has changed also—he is very short-tempered and at times I am
afraid of him. But can I blame him when I cannot fulfill my wifely
obligations to him? I have not willingly had him in my bed for over
a year, but Walter is a very forceful man, a very strong man. I
tried to talk to Daddy about my feelings, but he quickly dismissed
them as the feelings of a weak, spoiled child—and then scolded me
for remaining barren. Perhaps he is right.*

*I must close before someone comes in. As I read over the words I
have written they do seem foolish, but nonetheless, I shall give the
letter to Jewel and stay the course I set when I sat down at this
table. I want to tell you—while I still can—the effect you have
had on this woman's life.*

> *Love and good-bye,*
> *Laurel May*

Although the little bay slept standing up with his forelegs
hobbled, Coy slept not at all that first night on the trail
from Decatur. He lay in his blankets with his head on his
saddle and his eyes open while the fire slowly died out
beside him, the coyotes howled around him, and the
winter constellations came to twinkling life above him.

The letter was a torment to him—to know that Laurel May had been thinking about him all that time, just as he had been thinking of her; to read that she loved him. Those things caused him anguish because they rekindled a spark in him that he thought he had at last put out.

But the greater anguish Laurel May's words caused him was to read about her unhappiness—and her fear. Or was he misinterpreting her words?

Before daylight had even begun to break, Coy rolled his blankets, saddled his bay, and started westward again.

He pushed the bay across forty or fifty miles a day. He wanted to cover even more miles each day, but with the bay's only nourishment being dry plains grass he dared not. Even that pace seemed to be drawing twenty pounds of flesh a day from him.

Coy rode across the rolling hills of north Texas and then across the immense flat expanse of the Llano Estacado. He swung around the south end of the huge barbed-wire enclosed XIT Ranch until he crossed over into the Territory of New Mexico. Once in New Mexico he turned north, still holding a slight westward angle.

The farther west he rode, the higher and drier and colder it became. Also the bigger and less populated the country became. But big and lonely lands had been Coy's home for most of two decades, and he was as much at home in such places as the coyotes and antelope who lived there—and who at times stood motionless and stared curiously as he and the bay passed by silently.

Twelve days after leaving Decatur he caught sight of a faraway mound, seemingly poised right at earth's edge— Tucumcari Mountain. For the next two days the mountain would at times disappear behind a grass-covered swell of land. But it always reappeared, nearer and larger, than it had been the last time it was seen, until at one particular day's end he was almost at its very base, and in the town of

Redondo, New Mexico, set on the prairie between the mountain to the north and Redondo Mesa to the south.

The town was a small cowtown like so many others Coy had seen, but it seemed to be growing and prospering.

Coy boarded his bay in the livery stable on one side of the town's wide and dusty center street, paying the stableman extra money for extra-special care of the bay. Then he carried his saddlebags out into the twilight lit street, turned his coat collar up against the late-November highplains chill, and walked to the Mesa Hotel.

"I need a room," Coy said to the clerk behind the counter, "and a bath."

"Sign or make your mark here," the clerk said as he turned the big register around.

As Coy signed his name, he said, "I'm looking for some folks. They came from Texas this past spring. The talk around Decatur was they probably moved here. Big ranching family. An old man named VanHughes and a son-in-law named Davis."

"You've come to the right town, Mister"—the clerk turned the register back around and looked at it—"Bell."

"Where's their place?"

"Due south a few miles, right against the north side of the mesa. You got business with Mister Davis?"

"Maybe," Coy answered.

"Looking for work?"

"That's one thing I've never been guilty of," Coy said with a slight smile.

"Well . . . I was going to say if you are, then it's J.D. Davis you need to see."

"Thanks," Coy said. "Think I'll take that bath now if you'll heat me some water."

"Sure, mister . . . I was going to say, they'll both be in town tonight."

"Both?"

"Yeah—both J.D. and Walter Davis. There's a big

Thanksgiving dance down at the new Davis Lumberyard barn tonight. Everyone in the county will be there."

"The Davis Lumberyard?"

"Sure . . . the Walter Davis Lumberyard. He's providin' the eats and fiddlers and callers and all. It's more than just a Thanksgiving doins, sort of a christening of the new lumberyard, and I understand it's his and Mrs. Davis's anniversary, too. Like I said, everyone will be there, includin' me—as soon as I heat your bath water."

"Sounds like the Davises adjusted to New Mexico right quick."

"Guess so. They're big people. One of the biggest cattle operators . . . and the lumberyard . . . and they've already provided most of the money to build a new Methodist Church, too. Yes, sir, they *are* big people, all right. But good people. You know what I mean?"

Coy nodded. "Got an idea," he said. "How about that water?"

# CHAPTER 7

Coy soaked in the bathtub and shaved, put on the clean Levis and white shirt he had in his saddlebag, knocked the dust off his hat as best he could, then inspected himself in the mirror. He was surprised to see a man so thin and brown. With his high cheekbones, he thought he almost looked Indian. He removed the hat and saw that his ghostly pale forehead was even longer than it had been the last time he'd seen it. "You goddamn stupid cowboy," he said, with a grin to the mirror. Then he fastened the collar-button on his white shirt and walked out of his second-story room.

Coy had failed to ask the hotel clerk where the Davis Lumberyard was, and now the lobby was empty. He walked out onto the boardwalk and turned east. The street was deserted and dark, but he soon came to a place called the Maverick Bar that was lighted, so he opened the door and stepped inside, walked to the long bar, and ordered a shot of whiskey from the man standing behind it.

As the bartender poured his drink, Coy asked for directions to the lumberyard.

"Three blocks east and one north," the bartender said, "right on the northeast corner of town. You can't miss it, not tonight anyway."

"You going to the big dance, are you, cowboy?" a woman's voice said.

Coy turned his head and saw a woman walking alongside the bar toward him. She was tall, black-haired, and slender—pretty, in a gaudy, lusty sort of way—with dark eyes that matched her hair and cherry red lips and cheeks.

**40**

"The hotel clerk said everybody in the world was going. He sounded like it was sort of law that you *had* to go. Don't tell me you aren't going?"

"I don't think that law you were talking about applies to unescorted saloon girls—the Davises being upper crust and respectable like they are . . . But now if I was to be escorted by a gentleman like yourself—you *are* a gentleman aren't you, Mister—?"

"Bell," Coy said dryly. He hesitated, then said with a grin, "Don't be offended, ma'am, but I think I'd better go alone."

"No offense taken," the woman said, "but if the entertainment's not up to your standards there, you can always come back here . . . Mary's my name, room ten."

Coy tipped his hat and stepped back from the bar. "I'll remember that . . . Mary," he said, and started for the door.

The bartender had been correct—there was no way a man could miss the Davis Lumberyard, not on this night. Just a few steps after leaving the Maverick Bar, Coy heard the fiddles and the festivities and followed the sound straight to its source.

Horses wearing saddles and horses hitched to buggies and wagons were tied and hobbled all around the huge barn. The double south doors were open and the place was crowded with people. The platform for the musicians was at the far end, and only the fiddlers' heads and the head of the caller were visible above the crowd. Coy knew people were dancing in the center of the barn, although he couldn't see them. Placed around the outside walls were bales of hay for people to sit on and long tables full of meats, vegetables, cakes, pies, and punch. The barn smelled of new lumber, hay, and good food.

Children ran and played among the adults. There were women, young and old, in long, country-style dresses, some with bonnets and some without. There were men with white skin and town-type suits and shoes, and others with brown skin, high-heeled, spurred boots, and collar-buttoned shirts with no tie—of the same mold as Coy Bell.

As Coy stood and looked around a humorous thought came to him—I wonder if Walter and J.D. gave the Van-Hughes cowboys time off to come. Then he quickly decided it wasn't likely since it might cost the outfit a little money and give the cowboys the wrong impression of their proper station in life.

Coy was nervous again, knowing that at any minute he might see Laurel May. But he was determined to see her one more time, let himself know that she was okay, and then get out of her life for good. A crowded place such as this would probably be the ideal place in which to do what he needed to do, too. It would not seem unusual or improper for a man to exchange a few words with a lady here; even a drifting cowboy talking briefly to a proper, rich lady would not raise any eyebrows here. For Laurel May's sake, this was much better than his trying to catch her alone somewhere, where prying eyes and nosy neighbors might see them and start rumors and gossip that might bring her even more pain.

The fiddles suddenly fell silent and the caller was no longer calling his dance cadence. Instead, he was talking in a loud voice with a hand raised in the air—the caller's raised hand was all Coy could see from his vantage point—to help quiet the milling and chatting throngs of people: "Ladies and gentlemen . . . Ladies and gentlemen! . . . Let me have your attention for a minute, please!" When the milling came to a stop and the chatting all but died out he went on. "We are going to take a short break, but before we do, Walter Davis would like to say a few words to you. But before he does that, I think *we* should all give *him* a big hand. After all, he is the one responsible for all of us being here and having such a good time—and for having such a good, big, *free* feed!"

There immediately followed a long, loud round of applause, mixed with not a few loud cheers.

Coy stood at the rear of the crowd with his thumbs hung in his Levi pockets. He strained his neck once to look over the person's head standing in front of him, saw Walter Davis's smiling, bearded face briefly, then began scanning the crowd again for Laurel May.

"I just want to thank each of you for coming," Coy heard Walter saying, "and for accepting Laurel May and me into your fold like you have. But most of all, I want to thank Laurel May, on this our anniversary, for giving me the best five years of my life . . . and I want to give her this as a token of my love."

Coy heard the crowd ooh and aah and heard someone say, "Look at that necklace!"

The crowd started clapping and chatting again, and all those in the rear near Coy tried to position themselves so they could see what was happening on the platform. Coy strained his neck and tiptoed with the rest as the crowd grew suddenly silent, but he could see very little.

Then he saw Walter standing in front of a woman, fastening something around her neck. Then he leaned forward and kissed her, and they turned enough so Coy could see Laurel May's golden hair. Then he saw her hands slide around Walter's broad back and hold him in a loving—even passionate—manner.

Coy looked away, confused, even hurt. He knew the last round of applause was for the happy couple as they stepped, no doubt arm-in-arm, off the platform and onto the dance floor.

A lone fiddler stepped back upon the platform, picked up his fiddle, and said, "This waltz is just for Mr. and Mrs. Davis." Then the beautiful strains of the lone fiddle filled the barn while those who could watched the couple waltz and those who could not went back to eating or talking—talking, as far as Coy could tell, about what a happy couple Laurel May and Walter Davis were and what an asset to the community, no, the whole *country*, they were!

None of it made sense to Coy, no sense at all. What seemed to be going on here, and what seemed to be going on in Laurel May's world when she wrote the letter he got in Texas were two entirely different worlds. That letter had been written eight months ago, and things can change in a lot less time than that; Coy knew that. But . . . this?

Coy knew he should be glad Laurel May was happy. That kiss, even from the poor vantage point Coy had viewed it from, was not the kiss of a woman who thought God was punishing her because she could not love her husband. If it was all an act, it was a damn good one, thought Coy as he sat down on a bale of hay with the slow waltz still being played by the fiddler in the background of his mind.

Maybe just getting away from the ranch in Decatur was what had made the difference for her. Or maybe it had made a difference in Walter. Whatever, thought Coy as the fiddle stopped playing and people began to spread out and talk about other things, there's nothing for this two-bit cowpuncher to do but rattle his hocks out of here just as soon as he can.

"You stupid son of a bitch," he muttered to himself and laughed.

"I beg your pardon!" an older lady standing beside him said.

Coy tipped his hat. "I said, I've got to go dig a two-foot ditch, ma'am."

Then he heard someone near him say, "That's a mighty pretty necklace, Laurel May."

The older woman standing next to him said, "What a lucky woman you are, Laurel May. Twenty-nine years I've

been married to my Leroy, and I've only got one anniversary gift—and it was a milking stool!"

The people all around Coy laughed, and the next thing
he knew they were opening their ranks and making a lane.

"Mighty good shindig, Walter," a man standing right
behind Coy said.

"Thanks for coming, Jack. I hope . . ."

But no other words coming out of Walter Davis's
mouth—no other sounds at all—registered on Coy Bell's
brain for the next few seconds.

He stood like a marble statue as Walter and Laurel May
passed—Laurel May on Coy's side, so close he could touch
her, so close he could smell her perfume, so close the hem
of her dress brushed across his boot tops.

She looked right at him as she passed but did not say
hello. Did not nod her head. Did not do anything but walk
past like he was as invisible as thin air.

Coy was dumbfounded; he could not make sense out of
what was happening. That woman with Walter Davis . . .
*was not Laurel May!*

# CHAPTER 8

Coy walked away from the festivities in and around the Davis Lumberyard into a dark and cold November night where frost was already coating the grass. He walked to the north and away from town until he could no longer hear anything but the faraway mournful wail of a lone coyote. There he stayed, sometimes sitting and sometimes walking—but all the time thinking—until the night had passed and dawn was beginning to break.

For some reason, Walter had substituted this other woman—who *did* resemble Laurel May in size, hair, and eye color—for his wife. If the switch had been made after leaving Texas but before arriving in New Mexico, who would know the difference? . . . Leonard VanHughes for one. And, of course, Pete Jewel. And Maggie the cook. And brother J.D.

But Laurel had said in her letter that her father was blind and his hearing was going—fooling him might not be all that hard. Brother J.D.? He might go along with anything his big brother wanted to pull. But Maggie and old Pete Jewel would sure know the difference . . . *if* they were here!

One question kept forcing its way into Coy's thoughts, and each time it did it brought with it a stabbing, physical pain to his chest: Had Walter killed Laurel May somewhere between Decatur and Redondo? Was she buried somewhere in an unmarked grave, or had her body been discarded in a wash or thrown off an embankment somewhere like a cow's carcass and left for the wild animals to dispose of? Coy couldn't bear the thought that he had failed her. She had meant just exactly what she had said in her letter—she *was* afraid of Walter, and for good reason.

Coy went to his room in the Mesa Hotel, got his holster and old Colt .45 revolver out of his saddlebag, and strapped the holster around his waist.

Then he went to the sheriff's office, a block west of the hotel, and opened the door. Sunrise lit the top of Tucumcari Mountain and the rim of Redondo Mesa but had not yet touched the sleeping town itself or the layer of heavy frost that covered everything.

The sheriff was a small, slim man of about fifty-five, with gray hair and a gray mustache. Coy found him asleep on a cot in a small room off the office.

"Sheriff . . . wake up! What's your name?"

The man on the cot slowly awakened and sat up. "What in the devil do you want, mister? I don't let the drunks out until ten o'clock. Ever'body in town knows that."

"What's your name?" Coy asked again.

"Sheriff Joe Talbert . . . Now what do you want?"

"Get up and come with me and I'll tell you on the way."

"Just slow down a minute, cowboy," Talbert said. "On the way where?"

"The VanHughes Ranch . . . or maybe it's called the Davis Ranch."

"Okay. We got it figured out where it is you want us to go. Now you've got to give me a good enough reason to think I *ought* to go."

Coy thought it over a second and said. "How about the fact that Mrs. Davis has disappeared."

"Walter Davis's wife? Gone?"

"That's right," Coy affirmed. "Let's go!"

"Good God!" Talbert said as he pulled on his boots. "Of all people! How'd it happen? Where is she?"

"I don't know where she is or how it happened. All I know is that she's gone and we better get out there."

"Who are you and how did you hear about it?" Talbert

asked as he strapped on his gunbelt and slung his hat on his head.

"Name's Coy Bell, and what does it matter how I heard about it? Come on, Sheriff, we should have been halfway there by now!"

Sheriff Talbert led the way at a lope. They went four miles almost due south before passing underneath a wide gate that had a high sign across its top that read: "Davis/VanHughes Ranch, D/V Brand."

Coy wondered if Walter had recognized him last night at the dance. Probably not. After all, Walter had seen him for just a couple of minutes the day the horse bucked into the saddlehouse with him and broke his leg. And that had been well over three years ago. No, most likely Walter or J.D. would not remember Coy's face. Of course, if Maggie and Jewel were at the ranch, there was no doubt that they would know him.

A mile after passing underneath the sign, Coy and Sheriff Talbert trotted into the ranch headquarters. It was built at the base of Redondo Mesa, whose rimrock towered some seven hundred feet above the buildings, all of which were built of rock. There were at least a half dozen buildings in all, and all snuggled among towering cottonwoods whose leaves had all fallen off for the winter or were in the process even as the two riders stopped and hurriedly dismounted underneath them.

They tied their horses to a hitching post in front of the big house with the white rail fence around it and walked straight to the door, upon which Sheriff Joe Talbert knocked loudly and before which he stood and waited nervously.

It was Maggie, the cook and housekeeper, who opened the door in her usual solemn manner. She looked both men over, but gave no indication that she remembered Coy.

"Good mornin', ma'am," Talbert said. "I came as fast as I heard. Is Walter inside?"

"Of course I'm inside, Joe." Walter's voice. "Where else would I be an hour after sunup on a Sunday morning but home with my wife getting ready to go in to church. Come on in."

The sheriff shot Coy a piercing glance as he removed his hat and stepped over the threshold and into the spacious front room of the house where Walter Davis was sitting on a sofa smoking a pipe.

"What brings you out this early, Joe?" Walter asked.

"Well . . . ," Talbert fumbled for the words, "it's about your wife . . . but I thought I heard you say you were home with her getting ready for church."

"That's what I said, Joe. What's this about? Maggie, bring us some coffee, three cups. Sit down, gentlemen."

Talbert sat on the edge of the sofa folding his hat brim in his hand.

"I'll stand," Coy said.

"Laurel May!" Walter yelled. "Can you come in here? I think this concerns you in some way."

A pretty blonde-haired woman stepped from the hall into the room, wearing a dark blue, floor-length robe. "Concerns me? What on earth . . . Well, hello, Sheriff Talbert. What is this?"

"I . . . I'm sorry, Walter—Mrs. Davis—but this man came into my office this morning and said you, ma'am, had disappeared and—"

"Disappeared!" the woman said, incredulously. Then she laughed and said, "Well, Sheriff, as you can see that's hardly the case."

"Yes, ma'am," Talbert said.

"That's not what I said, Sheriff," Coy said evenly.

"You said she had disappeared, Bell! Don't deny it!"

"I didn't say *she* had disappeared. I said Laurel May Davis had disappeared—and she has! This woman is not

Laurel May. She is not Leonard VanHughes's daughter or Walter Davis's wife."

"I know you," the woman said, putting her hand over her mouth as if suddenly frightened. "You're the man who was at the ranch in Texas a few years ago with the broken leg—the one Walter let stay in the bunkhouse out of the goodness of his heart, and then you—you tried to attack me!"

Coy laughed. "Oh, you're something, lady—namely a real good liar. But you are *not* Laurel May!

"Get Maggie back in here, Sheriff," Coy insisted. "She—"

"Maggie *is* back in here."

Coy looked toward the kitchen door and there stood Maggie, holding a serving tray with three cups of coffee on it.

"I remember you, too," she said. "I even remember your name—something Bell. Laurel May never told me you had tried to attack her, but I could tell she was afraid of you."

Walter Davis was on his feet. "Neither one of you ever told me about this!" Then he looked at Coy. "*You* tried to attack my wife! Why you . . . I'll . . . ," and then a heavy fist landed in Coy's face, staggered him backward, and cut his cheek.

Instantly, Sheriff Talbert had hold of Walter's hand. "That's enough, Walter! I'll get him out of here. I didn't know."

Coy let the blood run down his cheek without bothering to wipe it off. He still spoke evenly, softly. "They're all lyin', Sheriff—all three of 'em. Ask 'em where Pete Jewel is. I'll bet anything he's not here. Is he, Walter?"

"Of course, he's not here. Pete wasn't our slave, and he didn't want to come to New Mexico, said he'd rather spend his last few years in Alabama."

"What about Laurel May's father?"

"He's on his bed, Sheriff," Walter said. "If you need to,

you can see him, but I'm afraid his mind comes and goes pretty bad at times. Sometimes, he's back in Alabama with Laurel's mother before the war."

"He's a very sick man, Sheriff," Maggie said.

"I know," Talbert said. "It won't be necessary to see him. I'm just sorry all of this happened, Walter . . . Mrs. Davis. I really got taken in by this man."

"Just get him out of here, Joe," Walter said, "and don't ever bring him back."

"You sure don't need to worry about that!" the sheriff vowed.

"Sheriff . . . ," the woman in the blue robe said, "I know this man must be sick, but he still scares me."

"Yes, ma'am," the sheriff said. "I can understand that, and I apologize again for bringin' him out here. Let's go, Bell, me and you got a lot of talkin' to do!

"I sure hope this hasn't spoiled your Sunday, folks."

"Don't worry about it, Joe," Walter said. "Just get him out of here. I'll be in town tomorrow to pay some bills and I'll drop by your office."

"Walter," Coy said just as cooly as ever, the blood now having crept down to his chin, "you got more than bills to pay . . . you've got *hell* to pay!"

# PART III

## THE CONSPIRACY

# CHAPTER 9

The front room in the ranch house was silent as Walter Davis stood at a window and watched Coy Bell and Sheriff Joe Talbert mount up and ride away.

Finally, Walter Davis said, "They're gone . . . for now."

"And I'm gone, too!" the lady in the blue robe said. "You said *nobody* would ever know the difference, you said—"

"I said we would pay you well and we will . . . but you'll do just what you're told to do. Now shut up!" Walter Davis said as he nervously pulled a broad hand over his heavy gray beard. Then he looked at Maggie, the tall, thin-lipped cook, and said, "Who was that, Maggie?"

Maggie sat her tray down. "My God, Walter, you don't even remember him? His name is Bell, just like I said— Coy Bell—and he's the one who's to blame for *all* of this!"

"You mean," said Walter twisting his head, "that that cowboy is the man—"

"He's the one you took pity on and let stay at the ranch just because he'd broken his leg. In return he ruined your marriage—and almost cost us the VanHughes fortune. While you and J.D. were off working three years ago that cowboy was weaving his web around your precious wife. Everything that has happened is *their* fault—Laurel May's and Coy Bell's fault."

"So what do we do now, big brother?" J.D. asked.

Walter turned his head to see J.D. standing beside the lady in the blue robe.

Walter looked at his younger brother a few seconds with contempt and then said, "I don't know."

"We're *so* close now," Maggie said. "The doctor said old Leonard could die at any time—any minute."

"And when he does, that fifty thousand dollars he has in the bank will be ours! Isn't that right?" the lady in blue asked.

"*Ten percent* of it will be yours, Katy, just like we told you," Walter said.

"And what about the ranch and all of the cows on it? I think—"

"You'll get ten percent of the cash in the bank and not another dime—just like we told you to begin with!" Maggie said.

"You can also have me," J.D. said. "One night with me and you'll be throwin' rocks at Big Brother."

"You don't think I *actually* go to bed with him, do you?" Katy said.

"Of course she doesn't!" Maggie exclaimed.

"I forgot—that's your job, right, Maggie?" J.D. asked with a grin.

"J.D.!" Walter yelled. "Leave Katy and Maggie alone. We've come too close to start tearing each other apart."

"Walter's right," Maggie said to J.D. bitterly. "Before Walter married Laurel May and took over the VanHughes Ranch Leonard was nearly broke. Now there's money in the bank and paid-for cattle in the pastures. Because of Walter, the VanHughes Ranch outgrew Decatur, so we came here where we can keep growing. Walter says we can double or triple the profits because we can use free grass. Here the Davis Ranch can become an empire!"

J.D. laughed wildly. "You and my brother deserve each other!" Then he stopped laughing and talked straight and cold. "But I'll tell you a few things . . . I'm in it with you all the way, because I'm greedy—just like the two of you are. But I don't blame Laurel May or that stupid lovesick cowboy, either. I don't blame Laurel May for runnin' away! She'd had all of Walter she could stand.

"But it ain't gonna be as easy as you think it will. You'd better listen to this and you'd better listen good. We may have to 'help' old Leonard 'pass on'—because that's *got* to happen right now! And we may have to kill Bell too, before he causes too much stink. Then, if we do all of *that*, and Katy here gets everything willed to her like we're planning, we'll lose it all and wind up in prison if Laurel May comes back—which she will, once she hears that Leonard is dead. That means that we need to find her *before* she comes back and . . . kill her too!

"And one more thing—we'd better *all* hope that you and Walter are dead wrong about there being a God and a heaven and hell!"

*"I am getting out of here!"* Katy said. "None of this was in our bargain. I'm not about to get involved in murder!"

Walter was across the room in a flash and had her arm in his strong grip. "Now you listen to me, you little harlot. You are going to do *exactly* as you are told. None of what J.D. was saying is going to happen. We've just got to keep our heads for a little while longer."

"Go to hell!" a defiant Katy said as she looked up at Walter Davis and into his cold, dark eyes. "I can see why the real Laurel May couldn't stand it anymore—and I can't either. Now let go of my arm, or I'll go have a little talk with Sheriff Joe Talbert."

The open hand came down hard across her face and drove her onto the floor.

"Now," Walter said softly, straightening his shirt, "go get ready for church."

# CHAPTER 10

Coy and Sheriff Talbert exchanged no words for the first two miles of the trip back to town. Then, as they rode in a slow trot against a cold north breeze Coy said, "I guess you could see how nervous they all were."

It was only after they were within sight of Redondo that Talbert responded to Coy's remark, and he did so without looking at the cowboy. "I'd be nervous, too, with a lunatic like you in my house."

"Sheriff . . . you've been a cowboy yourself, haven't you?"

Talbert now looked at Coy and said, "Yeah . . . till a couple of years ago when I was stupid enough to let myself get elected to this job."

Coy grinned. "I thought so—I can tell by the way a man sits a horse and handles his reins if he's a cowboy or not.

"Well, that's all I am, Joe—just a cowboy. I've never had much and never will. But like most of the breed, I've always had a good time and I've always tried to make an outfit a hand as long as I was drawin' their wages. Most of the places I've worked, I could go back to today and get hired on."

"I'm proud for you, Bell . . . Now why don't you just do that—go someplace where you've been and go back to punchin' cows instead of . . . whatever in the goddamn hell this is you're tryin' to pull here!"

"That's my point. Why would I ride in here and make any of this up? Hell, do you think I *want* trouble? Oh, I've gotten ahold of a little fightin' whiskey now and then, and I can't say that I've never woke up with a headache and looking out between jail bars. But that's been few and far

between, and the last time was many years ago. I'm a
pretty mellow fellow now—so why in the hell do you think
I'd be wantin' to make up a bunch of lies and cause myself
a passle of trouble?"

"You tell me, Bell—I can't figure it out!"

"I wouldn't."

"Why did you come here in the first place, then?"

Coy laughed a little, knowing how it was going to sound.
"I . . . I came to see Laurel May Davis."

"Why?"

"Dammit, Sheriff, I can't hardly understand it myself,
so there's no way I can explain it to somebody else. But,
Laurel May and I—the *real* Laurel May—got to be . . .
we . . . oh, hell, Sheriff! It doesn't matter why I came—the
fact is I did, and found out that Walter Davis has done
something with his wife and has someone else posing to
be her."

"Now *why* would he do that. And *where* would his real
wife be?"

"I'm afraid he's killed her and—"

"Good God, Bell! You're crazy as a locoed mare! I don't
even want to hear that kind of talk!"

"He killed her and got this other woman to take her
place. Leonard VanHughes may be so out of it he would
think any woman was his daughter as long as she said she
was. They're waiting for Leonard to die, so when he does
this other woman will inherit everything he has. Then, of
course, they'll probably fake this other woman's death
some way so everything will go to Walter."

"You must have had a lot of sleepless nights lately, Bell,
to dream all of this up," the sheriff said. "What about the
cook out there?"

"She's lying, too," Coy said, shrugging his lean shoulders. "I guess they're cuttin' her in on the deal, just like
they are the fake Laurel May. They say everybody has
their price . . . Not Pete Jewel, though. He's the old

caretaker I was asking about. Don't you find it strange that he's not there?"

"Nope," Talbert said with a shake of the head. "The way they told it makes sense to me. And I'll tell you what else makes sense to me—that if you go near that place again, I'll lock you up. And I don't want you scatterin' your shit all over town, either. I *do* have the authority to lock lunatics up, you know."

Coy thought about pulling up and letting the sheriff read the letter from Laurel May that he had stuffed in his shirt but decided against it, having no way to prove it was actually written by the real wife of Walter Davis.

"Guess you may be right, Sheriff—I'm just a crazy cowboy. Besides that, Walter *did* donate most of the money to build the new Methodist Church, didn't he."

"He sure did."

"So that means him and God are practically double first cousins, don't it?"

"Maybe not," the sheriff said, "but it sure doesn't mean he's a murderer and a thief, either." Then Talbert spurred his horse into a lope.

A couple of hours later, while the congregation of the Methodist Church was listening to Reverend Moore's fine sermon on tithing and charity, the front door opened and a man walked down the isle holding his hat in his hand. As the man approached the pulpit, Reverend Moore stopped his sermon and received a note from him.

Reverend Moore read the note, looked at the third pew on the left, and said solemnly, "Walter . . . I think you and Laurel May ought to go on home . . . It says here that J.D. rushed in to get Doctor Blackmore to go see about Mr. VanHughes."

Leonard VanHughes's funeral was held the very next day. His death was a tragedy but not unexpected. Many people attended, more out of respect for the Davises than for Leonard, as not many knew the old man personally. Mrs. Davis grieved and dropped a handful of dirt over Leonard's coffin after it was lowered into the grave. Mr. Davis was a great support to her.

After the ceremony, while people were still gathered in the cemetery to offer condolences, Coy saw his moment arrive. He saw the new Mrs. Davis standing by herself.

Coy walked up to her, removed his hat and, before he spoke, looked around. J.D. and Walter were talking with some other people about twenty feet away, and there was Maggie talking quietly to a group of older ladies. He smiled and said, "I'm sure sorry about your father, ma'am."

Only then did the woman see him. The color drained from her face as her eyes began darting back and forth, like a trapped animal's. "No need to be afraid, lady," Coy said very quietly, and then smiled as a couple walked by and spoke to her.

"What do you want?" she asked, her eyes scanning the crowd.

"Just want a chance to talk to you before Marshal Gates does."

"Who is Marshal Gates?"

"A friend of mine—who I ran into in Decatur—and who knows Walter and the *real* Laurel May," Coy lied.

"Please . . . ," she said, "I—I've got to go. Walter or J.D. might see us talking."

"They'll have to kill you, you know," Coy said quickly.

"No, you're crazy!"

"You're scared."

"You're damn right I'm scared!" she admitted in a loud whisper.

"I'll get you out and let you go . . . *if* you'll tell me what happened to Laurel May."

"They don't let me out of their sight!"

"You've *got* to find a way out of the house . . . Tomorrow night, about one or two in the morning, walk toward the east from the house and stay in the rocks next to the mesa."

"How can I trust you?" she asked.

By now Coy could see the real fear in her eyes, and not of him. "Who else can you trust?" he asked.

"I've got to go before they see us," she said.

"I'll be waitin' tomorrow night in the rocks east of the house," Coy whispered as she walked past him. "Don't try to pack anything or bring anything—just come and be ready to ride . . . *if* you're ready to talk. If you stay with them, you're dead, either by the law or by the Davis brothers. I think you know that now—I can see it in your eyes."

# CHAPTER 11

That night, Coy lay in his dark hotel room unable to sleep. He was not accustomed to dealing with lying, conniving people, not used to trying to prove to people that he was telling the truth—his truthfulness had never been questioned before. He had never felt so helpless. He had never been much of a fighter before, either. Oh, a few fistfights, sure, but he had never been the kind of a fighter it takes to succeed at great undertakings. If things happened not to suit him wherever he was, he had a simple and expedient means of remedying the situation—he rolled his bed and left. He had always been content to let the world go by as it was, and usually watched joyfully as it did so. But now—now there was no joy in his world, and he was filled with rage at the thought that people like Walter and J.D. Davis thought they could take whatever they wanted by might and force, that they were somehow above everybody else and beyond the rules of human decency—and of the law.

And then he thought of Laurel May's body decomposing in an unmarked grave or perhaps at the bottom of a bluff somewhere. *That* thought did it for him for the night. He put his hat on and decided to go have a drink at the Maverick Bar.

There were no more than a half dozen men and three women in the Maverick. He ordered a beer and carried it from the bar to a table in a dimly lit corner, where he sat drinking it alone.

"Well, hello there, cowboy—Bell, isn't it?"

Coy looked up. "Hello, Maverick Mary from Room Ten,"

he said as the tall, dark-haired woman pulled out a chair and sat down.

"You look kind of lonesome tonight," she said.

"Let's just say that those hotel room walls got to closing in on me."

"Would you . . . like to see *my* walls?" the woman asked with a flirtatious grin.

"Thanks," Coy said, "but I'm not in a buying mood."

The woman put her warm hand on Coy's leg underneath the table. "And I'm not in a selling mood."

"Mary!" someone from the bar yelled. "Come over here and have a drink with me."

Coy looked up and saw J.D. Davis leaning on the bar.

Mary scooted her chair back. "I'll be back as soon as J.D. leaves," she said.

Coy reached out and put his hand on her arm. "No," he said, "stay here."

"I'd better not—J.D. can get awful rowdy this time of night."

"You stay," Coy said, looking at J.D. Davis.

"Mary!" J.D. yelled again. "You come here . . . or I'm comin' over there."

"You stay," Coy said again, finishing his beer.

"Here he comes," Mary said.

J.D. walked over to their table in the dimly lit corner. "Bell? . . . Is that you? I thought so. If you're lookin' for trouble, I can damn sure give it . . ."

In a flash, Coy was on his feet and his empty beer mug was crashing against the side of J.D. Davis's face.

The mug shattered, and J.D. Davis melted to the floor like so much hot candle wax.

"Thanks for the offer, Mary," Coy said as he stepped over the prostrate body and walked toward the door, "but I think I can sleep now . . . After he wakes up tell him that it's just starting."

\*　　\*　　\*

Coy spent the next day riding out among a heavy growth of cedars on the rimrock of a canyon, resting up for the coming night, for it was this night that he was to meet the woman posing as Laurel May. Would she come? *Could* she come? Could she get away from J.D. and Walter? There was a good chance she could . . . for he intended to do everything he could to see that the Davis brothers had other things on their minds beginning about midnight.

But even if she came, would she tell him the truth? Did she know what had happened to Laurel May?

As the November moon arched across a cold sky, and most lanterns in town had been blown out, Coy came out of his cedar lair and headed for Redondo.

Once in town, he went straight to the new Davis Lumberyard and forced open the double doors to the barn. There, by the light of a match, he quickly made a sizable pile of lumber scraps against the east wall, underneath a rack holding new lumber.

Then he put a match to the pile of kindling and watched as the fire took hold. He watched, not with any joy, but with a certain amount of resignation. A man did what he had to do—and this ought to get J.D. and Walter away from the ranch long enough to give the woman a chance to get away from them.

In traveling to the ranch, he stayed off the road and amid the scattered mesquites, cactus, and rocks. As he topped a small rise two miles south of town he pulled up and looked back. The size of the blaze and the height to which the yellow flames reached was a surprise to him. But he only watched a few seconds with an emotionless expression before reining his bay around and riding south again.

Even though he could not see Redondo or even the flames of the burning lumberyard from where he waited for the woman among huge rocks at the base of Redondo Mesa, the northern horizon was glowing with an eery, yellow incandescence.

He had waited only perhaps a half hour before his bay snorted and pointed his nose to the west. Coy drew his .45, crouched behind a boulder, and waited in the cold moonlight.

Then he saw a form slipping from boulder to boulder. But he waited silently until he could tell . . . Yes, it was a woman!

"Over here," Coy said.

She approached cautiously. "Is it—"

"It's me . . . Coy Bell," he said, stepping out into the moonlight so he could be seen.

"So you came after all," Coy said as she stepped near.

"Please . . . You said you would help me get away!"

"Only if you're goin' to tell me the truth."

"I'll tell you everything I know . . . Please, let's go! If J.D. or Walter finds us . . ."

Coy stepped into the saddle and then held out a hand to the woman. "Put your foot in the stirrup and give me your hand. We'll ride double—and you can talk."

He pulled her up and she settled down behind the saddle. She was shivering.

"Put your arms around me," Coy told her. "After we put a few miles between us and the Davis brothers we'll stop and build a fire . . . Now start talking."

"My name is Katy Hill. I'm from . . . well, I'm from a lot of places, but I was working in a saloon in Amarillo when I met J.D. He made me a proposition—he asked how I'd like to make some real money by just pretending to be a rich man's wife for a while. He said they needed someone who looked like me—and someone they could trust. He said I could make enough money so I could do anything I wanted and go anywhere I wanted."

"I had most of that figured out," Coy said abruptly. "You were to pretend to be Laurel May until Leonard died and then everything would be willed to you. But what did they do with her?"

"Listen . . . they just told me she disappeared. They said she was no good. They even said I'd be doing the old man a favor by making him believe his daughter was still with him."

"Yeah," Coy said, "they're a kindhearted bunch, aren't they."

Katy Hill laughed. "They're the craziest and meanest bunch of people I ever met—including Walter's girl-friend!"

"Maggie?" Coy said.

"Yeah . . . Maggie."

"Maggie! . . . She's Walter's girlfriend? . . . That explains a lot!"

"She told Walter it was because of you that Laurel May wanted to end the marriage. Maggie, Walter, and J.D. said they had too much at stake to risk losing everything if Laurel May convinced her father to reclaim the ranch. I guess she started to make trouble after you left. That's why they think everything that has happened since is your and Laurel May's fault."

Coy laughed sadly and shook his head. "All we did was fall in love. Maybe that was wrong, but it wasn't something we planned to do. And Laurel May and I never once committed adultery—we both might have wanted to, but we didn't. When I left we never planned on ever seeing each other again. But she *never* loved Walter, even before I met her. I guess after that it just got worse and worse for her.

"I guess what has happened to Laurel May *is* my fault. If we hadn't ever met . . . But where is she now? They killed her, didn't they? . . . Because they were afraid she would tell Leonard she couldn't live like that anymore and they would all be sent down the road kickin' rocks."

"I don't know what really happened to her—not now. But when I got into this, I promise you I believed what they said about her being no good and just leaving. I know

now, though, how mean they are. They talked about maybe having to kill you and even the old man if he didn't hurry up and die—maybe they *did* kill him. I don't know."

"But you figured out they were going to kill you after the will was settled, didn't you?"

"Yes! I see that now—that's why I *have* to get away!"

"And I'm going to help you get away . . . but we're going to the Law—"

"No!" Katy Hill exclaimed.

"Not in Redondo, that would be too dangerous. We'll go back to Amarillo, where people know you, and we'll go to the Law there."

"But J.D. and Walter will—"

"You'll *never* be safe, no matter where you go, so long as they're free. You're smart enough to figure that out, Katy. You tell the truth in court, and they'll either hang or spend the rest of their lives in prison. It's the only way for you. If you stay they'll kill you, and if you leave they'll kill you— sooner or later. Tellin' the truth in court is your only way out."

Katy heaved a heavy sigh. "Maybe you're right. My God, I never thought any of this would happen. It was supposed to be easy—that's what they said. I'm scared, mister. I don't want to die."

"Laurel May was scared, too," Coy said. "The dirty bastards!"

Then, like a ghostly apparition, a mounted figure cradling a long-barreled shotgun emerged from behind a boulder no more than thirty feet in front of them. The bay stopped short and snorted.

"I warned Sheriff Talbert you might try to kidnap my wife." It was the voice of Walter Davis, speaking almost casually.

"Oh, my God!" Katy Hill muttered.

"Did you really think settin' that fire would fool us,

Bell?" It was J.D.'s voice behind them. "All it did was to tell us to watch and wait. Didn't I tell you, Walter?"

"Katy," Walter Davis said as he stepped closer to them, now holding the shotgun at waist level and pointing it directly at them, "I'm disappointed in you. I want you to know that I never wanted any of this to happen. But you should have stayed the course and kept up your end of the bargain."

"Both of you get off—slow and easy," J.D. said behind them.

Coy turned his head slightly and whispered to Katy, "Hold on to me real tight."

Then he dug his spurs into the bay's belly and screamed, "Go to hell!"

Walter Davis was knocked to the ground by the bay's shoulder.

A rifle shot rang out behind them and a bullet tore through Coy's hat brim.

And then the deep *ca-bloom* of the shotgun.

Coy's left side went numb and his hand involuntarily dropped the bay's bridle reins.

Katy Hill's grip loosened around Coy's waist. He heard her gurgle once, then she was gone.

More gunfire ripped the night, but Coy was only scarcely aware of it. Just as he was only barely aware of the bay running wildly underneath him as he slumped forward in the saddle and they began tearing through a heavy growth of mesquite.

# CHAPTER 12

Snow covered the ground and more was being carried on a cold and bitter wind as they buried Katy Hill beneath a tombstone that bore the name of Laurel May VanHughes Davis. Buried her beside Leonard VanHughes, and only three days after his interment. Buried her while an angry posse scoured the countryside for the cowboy Coy Bell.

Just after dark the posse came back to Redondo, cold, tired, exhausted, and empty-handed.

While the posse was returning to town, Reverend Moore was just leaving the grieving household at the Davis/VanHughes Ranch. He was standing at the open door with his hand on Walter Davis's shoulder. "Sometimes it's impossible to understand why some things happen, Walter. If it's any comfort to you, just remember that nothing in this world occurs without God's knowledge. Someday, through faith and prayer, the pain and anger will pass. Laurel is in God's hands now, at peace, where nothing else can harm her. And as for the deranged man who did this . . . Well, God has a way of bringing things full circle—in time I'm sure you will realize that. Good night."

"Good night, Odell—and thanks," Walter said sadly.

"Good night, folks," Reverend Moore said to J.D. and Maggie, who were sitting in the parlor.

Walter closed the door and turned around with his hands over his face. "My God," he said as he dropped his hands, "how did we ever get into this?"

"We got into this because of that cowboy's and Laurel May's sinful deeds," Maggie said, tight-lipped and bitter.

J.D. laughed. "We got into this, Maggie, because we

wanted to be rich—and *I* still do. Remember—I told both of you it might come to this. But, really, the way things have worked out couldn't be much better for us. Leonard died and left everything to Katy—or rather to Laurel May—she gets killed 'by that crazy cowboy' and everything goes to Walter. So in the end everything is turning out just like we talked about years ago back in Alabama."

"We never talked about killing people!" Walter said. "When Leonard made the proposition to me to marry his daughter and take over the business of running his ranch we never thought it would wind up like this. I brought you with me, J.D., and gave you the wagon-boss job you could never get on your own. And, Maggie . . . when you came to Decatur a little while after me and Laurel May were married, I gave you a job, too."

"I only did what I thought was right, Walter," Maggie Davis said. "You didn't love Laurel May and she was never a decent wife to you, even before that cowboy showed up. You and I deserved whatever happiness we could give each other. And you worked hard to build the VanHughes fortune up to what it is today—and it is rightfully yours. Ours."

"And Katy Hill, Maggie?" J.D. asked sarcastically.

Maggie's voice rose to a shrill pitch. "Katy Hill was a cheap harlot!"

"Besides, I didn't mean to kill her!" Walter insisted. "I just pulled the shotgun around and shot without thinking when I heard your shot. I thought Bell was shooting at me."

"Well, anyway," J.D. said as he stood up with a satisfied countenance, "let's just all remember who it was that pulled the trigger that killed her."

"And what about Leonard?" Walter asked, moving toward his brother.

J.D. smiled and shrugged. "You'll never know, will you?

Maybe he just died—or I might have put a pillow over his old face . . . but you'll never know one way or the other."

"And what about your smashing Katy's face in with that rock?" Walter yelled as he grabbed hold of J.D.'s shirt.

J.D. pushed the hand away. "*After* you had already killed her, Walter—I just made sure that if someone else from Texas showed up before we got her in the ground they couldn't tell whether she was Laurel May or not. The way it turned out it was unneeded." J.D. smiled smugly. "All it did was to make people around here hate Coy Bell even more. With him hitting me with that beer mug, and burning the lumberyard down, he already had most people thinking he was crazy—smashing Katy's face in convinced the rest of them."

"Now, boys," Maggie said, more calmly now, "let's not fight amongst ourselves. What's done is done, and I think it's about all over with now."

"Not till they find Bell and shoot him on the spot or hang 'im," warned J.D. "And then even when that happens, there's another thing you two seem to have forgotten."

"Laurel May," Maggie said.

"Yeah," J.D. said. "It's going to be sort of an embarrassment to all of us if she shows up here some day . . . But, don't worry. I've already contacted a man—a bounty hunter who can track a fly across flint rock. Wherever Laurel May is, he can find her—her and that nigger Jewel. *Then* it will be all over."

Coy Bell was aware only of the cold and the dark and the pain. He couldn't remember what had happened and he did not know where he was. He was not even sure of who he was.

He wanted to close his eyes and not fight the pain and the cold. But something inside him would not let go, as it finally must for a man to die. He slowly reached across his body with his right hand and felt the frozen blood on the left sleeve and side of his heavy coat. He felt down his arm until he reached his numb left hand. Half of it was gone, including the last two fingers. The part of the hand that was there felt like it was frozen solid. He tried to speak, but nothing more than a low grunt came out of his lips. He wiped the snow out of his eyes with his right hand only to have more of the dry, cold flakes quickly replace what he had removed. He ran his hand inside the coat and felt, without emotion, an exposed rib.

Somehow he knew, although he didn't know how he knew, maybe he heard it in the howling wind, that if he could but roll over onto his stomach and crawl forward a short distance he would be underneath a low, overhanging bank of dirt. Roll over and crawl something in his blood-thin brain screamed at him. Roll over and crawl!

Two days later at the close of day the posse rode into the barn of the DV ranch. Sheriff Joe Talbert was leading a little bay horse wearing an empty saddle. Walter and J.D. Davis dismounted stiffly and J.D. lit a lantern.

"I'm goin' to let everybody go home until the weather lifts, Walter," Sheriff Talbert said, his face shadowed in the dim lantern light. "The snow's gettin' too damn deep to ride through and everybody's wore out and half-froze. It must be damn near zero by now. As soon as we can, we'll start lookin' again. Chances are, Bell's dead. Judging from this blood on his saddle you must have hit him as hard as you thought you did. We may not find him until the snow melts, but sooner or later somebody will. Even if he's not dead yet, he can't survive out in this afoot, not even if he wasn't bad hit with buckshot. I know that's not much consolation to a man whose wife was just kidnapped and murdered, but it ought to help a little."

"Thanks, Joe," Walter said. "I know you and the rest of the men have done everything you could."

After the posse had disappeared into the swirling snow, Walter turned to J.D. and said, "What do you think?"

"I think he's dead. Talbert's right—it must be close to zero now and it'll get colder before morning. Can't see how any man, carrying a load of buckshot or not, could live long in this. We're through with Coy Bell, that's for sure.

"You unsaddle the horses and I'll go put 'em out some feed. Then we can go in the house, drink whiskey, and start plannin' our empire."

Walter smiled and nodded, rubbing a hand over his ice-covered beard. "Sure," he said, "why not. I'll see you in the house in a few minutes."

Walter Davis unsaddled J.D.'s horse first, put his saddle on a saddle rack in the saddlehouse, then started to loosen the cinches on his own mount. But suddenly the horse, and the little bay wearing the blood-splattered saddle, cocked their ears toward the darkened rear of the barn.

Walter Davis stopped and looked intently into the shadows for a few seconds, saw nothing, and reached down again for his latigo.

Now the little bay snorted.

"J.D.?" Walter said as he peered into the shadows. "What're you doing back here?" When no reply came forth from the shadows, Walter reached through the door of the saddlehouse and brought out his old Greener double-barreled shotgun. With both hammers cocked he moved slowly toward the rear of the barn, stopping at each stall to look inside.

"Don't turn around, Walter." A shaky voice behind him said. Walter Davis stiffened.

"Is that you, Bell?"

"What's left of me," Coy said, a .45 in his right hand, his left arm hanging limp at his side. He was dirty and bloody, his face bearded and wan, with eyes sunk far back into his head.

"You know there's no way out for you . . . You should never have come here."

"And you should have let me leave with Katy Hill . . . or killed me like you did her. What did you do with Laurel May?"

"Whatever happened to Laurel May she brought upon herself—"

"And what about Katy Hill?"

"That was an accident. That load of buckshot was meant for you—all of it. If you'd never come here she would be alive. It's all your fault!" Walter Davis screamed as he whirled around with his shotgun.

"Don't!" Coy yelled as his grip increased around the curved butt of the .45.

The .45 spoke a split second before the Greener. The Greener spoke a split second before it was centered on Coy Bell's chest.

Walter Davis died a split second before he fell face down in the barn.

A split second later J.D. Davis came running into the barn, but by then the darkness of a plains blizzard had swallowed up the cowboy Coy Bell and his little bay horse.

J.D. posted a reward for the capture, dead or alive, of his brother's murderer. Privately, he was banking on the bounty hunter named Buffalo finding Coy Bell first. Buffalo's instructions were to kill Coy, then to find Laurel May and Jewel.

*J.D.—No luck in hunting yet. Game scarce. Send more money. Waiting here for reply.*

*Buffalo*

*Buffalo—Disappointed in hunt and hunter. Here is more money. Reward for Bell increased to $2,500. I will pay like amount. Expect results soon.*

*J.D.*

*J.D.—Not easy job. Stories about Bell all over the place, but none amount to anything. Still no tracks of other game. I am the best. Send more money. Waiting here for reply.*

*Buffalo*

*Buffalo—It's been over a year and a half. No more money in advance. Have lived up to my end—you haven't. Must hunt on your money from now on. If game is spotted, get in contact.*

*J.D.*

# PART IV

## A SECOND CHANCE

# CHAPTER 13

Coy Bell rode to the top of a rocky hill overlooking a narrow creek in the Sierra Madre range in the state of Chihuahua. He stepped off the long-legged gray horse he was riding and stood under the blistering sun to look out over a rocky land that was parched and thirsty.

Squatting in the gray's shadow he rolled a smoke, stuck the cigarette between his thin lips, and rasped a match across a metal concho on his leggins. As he held the match to the end of the cigarette, he glanced at the two stub fingers on his left hand. They were healed now, as was the awful scar on his left rib cage, but served as a constant reminder of what had happened in Redondo, New Mexico, two years earlier.

He took his hat off and wiped the sweat from his forehead with a shirtsleeve. Then movement below him caught his eye, as well as the eye of the gray who lifted his head and pointed his ears.

Slowly, Coy snuffed out the cigarette, stood up, and pulled the Winchester carbine from his saddle boot. Then he sat back down in the gray's shadow, eyes glued to the rocks below.

The gray dozed, but Coy did not. Ten minutes passed by quietly with the only movement that of a slowly circling buzzard overhead, a long green lizard scurrying from the shade of one rock to another, and the sleeping gray shaking his head now and then to ward off the gnats around his eyes and nose.

A rider appeared below. Then another.

"Well," Coy said to no one, "looks like my Yaqui Indian

friends are wanting back in the beef business again." He
put the Winchester to his shoulder, rested his elbows on
his knees for support, put the blade of the front side on
the lead Yaqui's head, exhaled, held his breath, and began
squeezing the trigger. But he stopped and lifted his cheek
off the rifle butt and grinned. Then he put his cheek back
against the rifle butt, put the front blade two feet above
the lead Yaqui's head, and fired.

When Coy's bullet plowed into the rocks just above the
lead Yaqui's head the pair of them whipped their horses
into a run. By then Coy had levered another .44-40 car-
tridge into the Winchester's chamber, and no sooner had
the Indians' horses started running than his second bullet
ricocheted off a sandstone rock only inches in front of the
lead pony.

The Yaquis pulled rein, turned their horses quickly
around, and whipped them into a run in the opposite
direction. Again Coy's Winchester split the scorching Mexico air as he planted a bullet again only inches in front of
the lead horse.

The Yaquis pulled up, confused, jabbering in Spanish.

"Yaquis!" Coy yelled, standing up and holding the rifle
above his head. "You savvy vamoose?"

"Savvy! Savvy!" one of the Indians below yelled.

"Pronto! Pronto!" Coy returned, as he snapped the rifle
to his shoulder and fired twice more in rapid succession,
his bullets splattering into the rocks only inches above the
Indians' heads and sending them down the narrow creek
as fast as their ponies could run.

As Coy slipped the rifle back into his saddle boot he
yelled. "You shouldn't sneak up on a man like that, Henry.
He might get the wrong idea about your intentions."

Henry DeBois stepped out from behind a rock, leading
his horse and wearing a wide grin as he squinted in the
bright sunlight. "Wasn't exactly sneakin' up on you, Ben.

Just didn't want to disturb a man at his work . . . You could've killed both of them damned Yaquis."

Henry was foreman of the Sierra Madre Cattle Company, owned by businessmen in Philadelphia. He was a hard man handling hard men doing a hard job in a hard country—making the ranch pay in spite of poor cattle prices, scarce rainfall and grass, and marauding Mexicans and Yaquis.

"I could have killed 'em, I guess," Coy said. "But I don't figure they'll be back huntin' for beef on this outfit for a while. I thought that was the main idea."

"The trouble is, they *will* be back, Ben."

"We can't kill 'em all, Henry. And hell, they gotta eat, too, just like me and you. Now if you don't like the way I'm doing my job—"

"Hold on a minute, Ben," Henry DeBois said. "I never said that. You're just the kind of man I want—good with a rope *and* a gun, and quiet about it. I hired a couple of new fellers today, and I just hope they will be half as good as you are, but they're young and cocky, not like you.

"You're the kind of man who could be runnin' an outfit back in the States, but here you are in Mexico damn near a year, drawin' the same poor wages as men who aren't half the hand you are. Like I said, it's not that I'm not glad you're here or have stayed so long—it just don't figure unless . . ."

"You're not askin' are you, Henry?"

"No, Ben," Henry said, shaking his head, "I ain't askin' and I never will. Most of the cowboys on this outfit are here because they're runnin' from something back in the States, but that's their business so long as they do their jobs while they're here. And you have damn sure enough done yours."

"And I've got some more of it to do before dark," Coy said as he mounted the gray. "See you at camp tonight." Then he put the gray on a steep trail that led down toward the creek and they disappeared over the rim, leaving Henry DeBois standing beside his horse.

It was almost dark when Coy rode into camp—a noisy camp where the liquor was already flowing freely. There were seventeen men at the camp, counting the two new hands Henry had hired today, plus the cook and horse wrangler. Most of them were good cowboys as far as their work went, but they were also the kind of cowboys with an untamed streak in them—a penchant for whiskey and wild living—that had gotten them into one sort of trouble or another back in the States. But this kind of devil-may-care cowboy was what Henry DeBois and the Sierra Madre Cattle Company needed. In fact, Henry DeBois was convinced that a man with mild manners and an untroubled past could not handle the sort of double-duty cowboy-gunhand his work on the Sierra Madre required. Every man was paid his wages in cash. Many of them went by only one name; most—like Coy—picked a name at random instead of using their own.

"Better come and git it before it's all gone, Ben," Scruggs, the cook, said as Coy rode the gray past the adobe shack toward the large rock horse corral.

"What Scruggs means, Ben," a wiry cowboy called Nails said, "is that you'd better come git it before it gits over what was ailin' it and walks outa camp."

Coy smiled and lifted his hand, but went on to the horse corral where he unsaddled the gray. Then he roped Blake, his own little bay, out of the horses in the corral and saddled him before going to eat. It was something he did every time there was a new man coming to the outfit—saddle his little bay and be ready to ride. You could never tell—never be too sure. He knew he was one of the most wanted men in the whole Territory of New Mexico—wanted for the killing of Walter Davis, which he did in self-defense, when Walter had whirled around with his shotgun.

But he was also wanted for the brutal murder of Katy Hill, who everyone supposed was Laurel May Davis. The thought of even being accused of killing a woman repulsed him. It sickened Coy to know that people thought he was a woman killer. But how could he ever prove otherwise? The only people alive who knew who really killed Katy Hill were J.D. and Maggie, and it was a cinch they weren't going to tell the truth.

Maybe someday he would go back and kill J.D. He was as involved in whatever happened to Laurel May as Walter was . . .

Laurel May—his Sunshine. Where *was* she? Dead, no doubt—he accepted that. Somehow his killing Walter Davis made her murder easier to face. But it would always bother him that he would probably never know where they buried her. Had his and Laurel May's feeling for one another caused all of this? Was that possible? What they had felt was wrong because she was married; they both realized that and said good-bye. Now Laurel May was dead, Walter was dead, a woman named Katy Hill was dead, and he was an accused woman killer with a price on his head and no way to prove his innocence.

"It's a hell of a way to run a world, Blake," Coy whispered to the horse as he patted him on the rump. Then he hobbled the horse and walked toward the cook shack and the bright camp fire burning in front of it.

Coy filled his tin plate with beef and beans inside the shack and carried it outside. He chose a place back a ways from the fire and the circle of loud men gathered there, sat down cross-legged with the plate in his lap, and began eating in silence.

As he ate he listened to the loud cussing and boasting of the men—boasting about their or someone else's prowess with rope, gun, or woman.

Then he was aware of eyes upon him. He looked up to

see one of the new hands Henry DeBois had hired holding a bottle of whiskey in his hand and staring at him.

The new hand was not much more than a kid, probably no more than twenty, although he was big, with cold, dark eyes and a pointed nose. He leaned over and said something to the other new hand, who was smaller and a little older. They seemed serious now. There seemed to be an argument of some kind, concluded shortly with nods and smiles and more stares at Coy Bell.

"Hey, you!" the younger, bigger hand said. Coy kept his eyes on the plate in his lap.

An older cowboy, named Giles, walked slowly by Coy and said, "Be careful, Ben. That feller's lookin' for trouble."

"I can tell, Giles," Coy said. "I'll just finish eatin' and go back to the horse corral. Do you know who he is?"

"Fletcher, is all I know. Killed a couple of men who were too drunk to find the hammer on a Colt. Now he thinks he's the toughest son of a bitch that's ever been split up to the crotch."

"Thanks, Giles," Coy said as he stood up with his plate and walked to the fire. There he dumped the scraps of food into the fire and dropped the plate into a large pan of hot water sitting over some coals beside the fire.

"I was talkin' to you a while ago," Fletcher said.

Coy looked at him, saw the whiskey red of his face and eyes. "So talk," he said.

"I saw your left hand. Seen them missin' fingers. Seen a wanted poster with a man on it that looked like you, and it said he had two missin' fingers on the left hand—like you do. Said he had a bad scar on his left side, too."

"That so?" Coy said.

"Said this man was named Coy Bell and he was a woman killer."

Coy's face reddened. "Poster's wrong," he said.

"A woman killer is a yellow bastard in my book,"

Fletcher said. By now everyone in camp was listening to them.

"Reckon there's not a man here who wouldn't agree with that . . . Now I think I'll go check on my horse," Coy said, stepping through the men.

Fletcher stepped in Coy's path. His left hand gripped the neck of the whiskey bottle, and his right dangled next to the butt of his holstered gun.

"Now look, son," Coy said, "you've made your point. You're a dangerous man and Coy Bell better look out if he ever comes across you. Now why don't you have another drink and enjoy the rest of the night. We got cow work to do in the mornin', so I think I'll check my horse and then get in my bedroll." With those words, spoken softly, Coy walked away from Fletcher, the fire, and the group of men there.

"I say you're Coy Bell," Fletcher said, "a yellow, god-damned woman-killin' son of a bitch."

"Hold it!" Henry DeBois said as he came out of the cook shack. "This has gone far enough. Fletcher, roll your bed and ride outta here."

"Why are you protectin' this woman killer, DeBois?" the young gunhand said.

"I don't know much about Ben, but I know enough to know he's not a woman killer," the foreman said.

"I got the poster in my saddlebags to prove it," Fletcher said. "And I'm callin' his hand right here."

"Fletcher! I said—"

"It's all right, Henry," Coy said, as he pushed his hat back with his right thumb. Then he said to Fletcher, "Now, son, one of us can die right here, maybe both of us. Or we can both go about our business and be alive to make that big circle Henry's got planned for us in the mornin'. I'd rather make the circle, how 'bout you?"

"Are you Bell?" Fletcher asked.

"Yeah," Coy said. "I'm Coy Bell. I killed Walter Davis but—"

"And his wife," Fletcher said.

"She wasn't his wife and I didn't kill her. Now, son, what about that circle in the mornin'? We both goin' to make it with Henry?"

Fletcher hesitated, looked nervously at his partner, then looked at Coy Bell and made the awaited announcement. "No."

"Then let's see who's not going to need a horse in the mornin', son. Henry—if it's me, I want you to have that bay horse and my saddle. Fletcher, it's gettin' late. I see the fear startin' to build in your eyes, boy. That's a bad sign for you. Why don't you have one more big old swaller of that panther piss and see if you don't want to forget the whole thing."

Fletcher slowly lifted the bottle to his mouth and took his drink.

Coy smiled. "See you fellers in the mornin'," he said, and turned and walked toward the horse corral.

"Ben!" Henry DeBois shouted.

Coy whirled around as Fletcher's gun exploded.

Fletcher shot first, but his bullet went wide.

Coy's bullet exploded the whiskey bottle in Fletcher's hand before passing through the would-be gunfighter's neck.

Coy's gaze shifted to Fletcher's partner, whose own gun hand was resting on the butt of his weapon. "What'll it be, son?" Coy said to him in an unhurried tone. "You joinin' your partner down there or makin' that circle with the rest of the men in the morning?"

Color drained from the young man's face as his hand jerked away from the curved butt of wood and steel like it had been burned.

"Thanks," Coy said as he slid his Colt back into leather and turned away.

"Looks like Fletcher's horses can go into the extra string, Frank," Henry DeBois said to the horse wrangler.

Coy was on his little bay, riding out of camp, when he stopped beside Henry and looked down at him. "Sorry, Henry. For what it's worth to you, I didn't kill that woman."

DeBois shrugged his lanky shoulders. "Never thought otherwise, Ben. I want you to stay."

"No," Coy said with a long, deep breath. "I'm movin' on. If I'm going to have men gunnin' for me, I'd just as well be back in the States where I feel more at home. I didn't think it mattered one way or the other, but just now, when I thought I might die, I was wantin' to be in America. She's my home—I reckon I'll live and die there. Good-bye, Henry."

# CHAPTER 14

An old, colored gentleman with a bowed back leaned on the handle of a plow pulled by a single mule. It was a blistering hot day. The field was dry, and the plow broke out big clouds of earth instead of turning over moist soil.

The old man pulled a rag from a pocket of his frayed overalls, removed his floppy hat, and wiped the sweat from his head and face. Then he poked the rag back into a pocket, slapped his floppy hat back on his head, and said to the mule, "Gitup, Sara. This ground is harder than last week's biscuits, but we cain't waits no longer for a rain." He glanced at the corn in the next field. "And that po' corn cain't wait much longer neither . . . Gitup now, I said . . . Come on heah, girl, let's get to work! . . . It's gotta be did."

The mule pushed against her collar, and finally the plow began to rip clods out of the earth again. Then the old man staggered, pulled the mule to a stop, and leaned on the plow handle before collapsing onto the parched ground.

"Jewel!" a woman in a big sunbonnet and long calico dress yelled from the doorway of a sod house close by. "Jewel!" she screamed again as she gathered up her skirt and started running to where the old man was lying in the field.

The woman lost her sunbonnet during her flight, allowing her long, yellow hair to stream out behind her.

By the time she arrived at the plow the old man was on his feet, leaning on the plow handle again.

"Jewel, you're getting too hot out here," she said.

"No, Miss Laurel," Jewel said, "I ain't gettin' too hot . . .
I was just alookin' for somethin' on the ground. That's all
I was doin'."

"You go get a drink and sit in the shade for a while,"
Laurel May said with some authority.

"But, Miss Laurel, this field has gots to be plowed
and—"

"I'll plow while you rest," she insisted.

"But, Miss Laurel, it ain't right that you—"

"Jewel, will you stop it!" Laurel May said in exasperation.
"I am *not* a dainty southern belle anymore. I'm a sharecropper in Nebraska who can't afford to lose a crop. I've
got sharecropper's hands and a sharecropper's skin. I can
milk a cow and slop the hogs . . . and I can plow, too! So
you go get in the shade."

"Awright," the old man finally conceded, "but just fo' a
few minutes . . . Maybe them clouds beginnin' to gather
yonder will bring rain tonight." Then something else
caught his eye and he pointed a thin, crooked finger
toward the west. "Look at that big dust cloud goin' way up
in the air yonder past them hills."

"I guess another trail herd is passing by, headed north,"
Laurel May said as she unwrapped the mule's reins from
around the plow handle.

"Miss Laurel, you ever wonder if—"

"—if any of those trail herds ever have VanHughes or
Davis cattle in them? What difference would it make if
they did!" she said bitterly. "I'm sure Daddy disowned me
long ago. There is no going back—not for me, Jewel."

"But Mistuh Leonard loves you, Miss Laurel."

Laurel May laughed sadly and shook her head. "Then
he had a funny way of showing it. No, I expect him and
Walter are getting along just fine without me. Daddy has
the son he always wanted in Walter—and Walter has his

ranch. Daddy could never see that a woman has to have more."

Now it was old Pete Jewel who laughed sadly. "You call this more?" he asked, looking around the dry quarter-section farm with the old sod house and barn sitting forlornly in an open field.

"If you're asking me if I have any regrets, the answer is no. Besides, regrets won't get this field plowed or bring a crop in."

"But, Miss Laurel, you cain't do it all. I do what I can, which ain't much, and someday I won't be heah at all. You need a man . . . Why won't you let that Mistuh Gibbons who owns the mercantile in Sidney court you like he wants to. He's a good man and—"

"I don't need a man, Jewel . . . Not like you mean, anyway. You and I will make a crop this year. And if you weren't here, I'd do it alone. I don't need anybody! Now, will you please go sit in the shade for a little while?"

Then Laurel May slapped the mule's rump with the lines and the plow lurched forward as she tightly gripped the handles, leaving Pete Jewel to stand alone in the field for a few seconds before walking unsteadily to the small pond close to the house where grew the only tree on the farm.

"Damn it, Sara, you can walk a little slower can't you!" Laurel May said as the sweat ran down her back and streaked through the dust collected on her face. Had she made a mistake by leaving? Had she broken her father's heart? What if it didn't rain? What if they didn't make a crop this year?

Then through the tears welling in her eyes, she saw the rising spire of dust again from the passing trail herd. Damn you, Coy Bell! she thought. You probably don't even remember my name. You're out there cowboying somewhere without a care in the world. I wish I'd never met you!

"Damn it all, Sara!" she said as the tears rolled down her cheeks and as the plow tore through the hard crust of earth jerking and snatching her this way and that.

Pete Jewel sat in the shade of the tree by the pond and watched Laurel May following the plow. Why was she so hardheaded? Didn't she know that someday she was going to be all alone? It broke his heart to see what was happening to her. Couldn't she see that her youth and beauty were passing her by just as surely as the trail herd at the bottom of that column of dust in the west was passing by, never to return again?

Three miles west, the trail herd contained 1,500 head of cattle bound for the Black Hills of South Dakota, there to be fattened on reservation grass by the Sioux Indians.

While Laurel May plowed in the hot afternoon Nebraska sun, word passed around the herd from cowboy to cowboy: "There's a little creek up ahead to water-out the herd. We'll let 'em all tank up and then we'll move them back aways and make camp for the night. Tomorrow afternoon we'll cross the Platte and be in the hills inside of a week."

Later that afternoon the cowboys with the herd sat crosslegged on the ground eating beef and beans and sourdough biscuits out of tin plates. The trail boss, a slim, quiet, ever-vigilant man with pale blue eyes, named John Denny, finished eating, got up, and dropped his plate into a metal washpan filled with steaming water. Then he walked off by himself to roll a cigarette and look at the cloud bank in the west. As he stuck the cigarette between his lips he absently rubbed the ends of the two stub fingers on his left hand with his thumb.

He lit the cigarette and walked back to the circle of cowboys. "Boys," he said, "I've been watching those clouds all afternoon. They've just hung back in the west and built, but they'll start movin' before long and when they do I've got a feeling things might go to poppin' around here. If I were you, I'd saddle my best night horse and keep my second best on the stake. I think we'd better double up the guard tonight, too."

The men said little, but almost to a man they nodded their heads in agreement with their boss's orders. John Denny had taken over a situation in which many men would have failed, and he had handled it to everyone's satisfaction. He had not been trail boss when they left Texas, just a hand. But the original boss had come down sick along the way and had to stay behind, appointing John Denny to take his place—partly because he was one of the oldest cowboys in the crew and partly because he was also one of the best. John Denny reluctantly accepted, and lead mostly by example. He was a quiet man who stayed by himself a lot and when they met strangers along the trail, he usually appointed someone else to visit with them and find out what, if anything, they wanted.

Denny had been correct in his assessment of what would happen once the cloud bank in the west stopped building and passed over. Things did indeed "go to poppin' " as he had predicted. There was a small flood and a small tornado. Trees were uprooted along the creek, the bed wagon overturned, and the herd scattered like a covey of quail kicked out of the underbrush.

It was a long and scary night, but by four in the morning most of the steers had been thrown into a manageable herd again and the bed wagon uprighted.

At the first crack of daylight the cattle were passed between Denny and another cowboy for a count. They both came up with the same tally—1,376 head. One hundred and twenty-four steers were missing.

"Boys," Denny said to the men after he had called them all together, "we'll eat a bite right quick and then start tryin' to gather our steer out of these farms and homesteads. Bob, you and Lyle better stay with the herd here. Ken, why don't you take half of the men and make a big circle around thataway." He indicated with a sweep of his hand a circle that would start toward the south, swing west, then come in from the north. "I'll take the other men and go this other way. Get every hoof you see that's alive and wearing a T Slash brand, and get an ear off any dead ones you come across so we can account for as many as possible when we make delivery in the hills."

It had been an exhausting, frustrating day for Laurel May. Jewel had been too weak to get out of bed, and she had run herself ragged trying to keep cattle out of the cornfield.

Now it was getting late in the afternoon, and as she was walking toward the barn to milk the cow, she saw three more steers in the corn. "I'll be damned!" she said. "We finally get a rain that might save the corn and now those steers want to eat it all or knock over what they don't eat!"

She carried the bucket back into the house and started out the door with her broom. But then she saw what was the last straw for her for the day: a cowboy running through the muddy cornfield on a horse, roping a steer! She carried the broom back into the house and came out running with a shotgun.

She stopped under the tree beside the pond and yelled at the cowboy, now off his horse and in the process of tying down the steer, "Get out of that cornfield! Haven't your steers done enough damage without your running through it too!"

But the cowboy paid her no mind, so she took off toward him, running between rows of short corn. She stopped when she was a hundred feet away and fired into the air. But she accidentally discharged both barrels at once without the butt of the gun firmly against her shoulder. She staggered backward, got her heels entangled in a cornstalk, and fell on her seat in the mud.

The shotgun's blast spooked the horse, and he started bucking at the end of the thirty-foot catch rope.

The cowboy whirled around with his .45 drawn and full-cocked, trying at the same time to keep from getting run over by his horse or tangled up in the rope and to see who in the world was doing the damn shooting!

He saw a yellow head of hair catching the slanting rays of the sun among the short cornstalks and heard a woman crying. Though he did not holster his Colt he did relax his grip on it somewhat.

"Are you hurt?" he yelled.

When the reply came back a belligerent, "NO!" he slipped the gun back into his holster, calmed his horse, took the rope from the steer's head, coiled his rope up, and tossed it over his saddle horn.

Then he got back into the saddle and trotted up to the place where the woman was still sitting in the mud and crying.

"Listen, lady," he said, "you ought to be more careful with that shotgun! Just what in the hell were you trying to do anyway?"

Laurel May put her hands in the mud and pushed herself up. "I'll tell you what in the hell I was—" She stopped, frozen in mid sentence. A pair of muddy hands came to her mouth. "Coy? . . ." She barely whispered his name.

"My . . . God!" Coy muttered from his saddle in utter disbelief, unable to move.

It was several seconds before he was able to swing his leg over the cantle of his saddle and step to the ground. Even then he moved slowly and cautiously. "Sunshine? . . . My God!"

"Oh, Coy . . . Coy!" Laurel May cried as she flew into his arms.

"How can this be, Sunshine?" he whispered as he wrapped his arms around her.

# CHAPTER 15

"Coy . . . Coy . . . ," Laurel May whispered over and over as she buried her head in his chest. "Where have you been?"

"I thought . . . I thought you were dead and buried in an unmarked grave somewhere, Sunshine," Coy whispered as he stroked her golden hair. "How did you wind up in Nebraska?"

Laurel May lifted her head. "Buried? Why—"

"Don't you know what all has happened?" Coy asked in disbelief.

With a puzzled expression, Laurel May shook her head. "What *has* happened?"

"We'd better go sit down somewhere, Sunshine," Coy warned.

"Let's go into the house," she said, stepping back from his embrace. "I've got some coffee on the stove, and I'll fix supper for you! And we can talk and tell each other everything. Oh, Coy . . . let me touch you again to be sure this is really happening . . . Oh, but don't look at me!" She turned her face away. "I look like a field hand—an *old* field hand."

Coy put his hand under her chin and turned her mud-smeared face so he could look into her blue eyes. "You're even more beautiful than you were five years ago."

She lifted her face to kiss him.

Coy put his fingers on her lips. "Not now, Sunshine—not until I've told you everything . . . by then you may not want to kiss me. I'm a wanted man now—an outlaw with a price on my head and nothing but the gallows waiting for me if they ever take me in alive."

"No, Coy," she said knitting her brow, "I don't believe that . . . How—?"

"Let's go to the house, Sunshine, and get that coffee—I'm afraid you're going to need it . . . Maybe something stronger." Then as they walked side by side out of the cornfield Coy shook his head. "Do you know what a shock it is to see you? For two years I've thought you were dead. God, if I'd only known!"

Coy stopped at the pond close to the sod house, slipped the bits out of his horse's mouth, and let him have a drink. Then he hobbled the horse in front of the austere dwelling with its sagging dirt roof and dead grass hanging limp and brown from the seams of the sod bricks.

Chickens scratched for grubs in front of the house, and a cow bawled from the lean-to cowshed fastened onto the small sod barn close by.

"Just about milking time," Laurel May said with a twinkle in her eye.

"You? Milk?" Coy asked incredulously.

"I sure do—and I'm darn good at it, too."

"Somehow I can't picture that . . . no more than I can picture you living here," Coy said as he loosened the cinches on his saddle.

"At one time," Laurel May said, "I never would have believed it either. Now I'd believe nearly anything."

"Well, Sunshine," Coy said as he removed his hat before stepping across the sod-house threshold, "you just remember you said that when I start telling you what happened in New Mexico."

They stepped inside the nearly dark house. As Laurel May lit the lantern on the table, she said, "Jewel, look who's here!"

The old man sat up on the edge of his bunk.

"Why, Pete Jewel, you old black devil!" Coy exclaimed as

he stepped across the earthen floor to grasp the hand extended to him below Jewel's thoroughly surprised face. "I should have known you'd be with Laurel May!"

"Mistuh Coy! Where in thunder did you come from?"

Coy looked around the one-room dwelling, scarce of nearly any modern convenience save for the wrought-iron Home Comfort Range fueled by the cow chips stacked beside it. "Better pull a chair up at the table with me and Laurel May, Jewel, and you'd better take a deep seat, 'cause it's going to be a rough ride."

And a rough ride it was, for both Jewel and Laurel May. An unfathomable, grievous ride to learn that Leonard VanHughes was dead—maybe murdered, maybe not, Coy didn't know. To learn that when Coy got to Redondo there was another woman posing as Laurel May and that Coy had been sure the real Laurel May was dead. To learn that Walter had killed Katy Hill—Laurel May's imposter—with a close-range blast in the back from a shotgun as Katy was on a horse behind Coy and that the shotgun blast had almost killed Coy—he held up the stub fingers on his left hand and raised his shirt to show them the awful scar on his rib cage. To learn that Coy had somehow survived the wound and zero weather to come back in a weakened, feverish state to kill Walter.

"I might have killed him even if he had not whirled around with his shotgun," Coy admitted. "But it really doesn't matter how it happened, I'm wanted for Walter's murder . . . and even worse, for the murder of Katy Hill, who's buried under a tombstone with your name on it, Laurel May. I'm the most wanted man in the whole Territory of New Mexico, and posters are spread all over the West, telling what a brutal killer I am. Some men would shoot me on sight for the twenty-five-hundred-dollar dead-or-alive reward and others would shoot me because they think I'm a woman killer.

"Still others would shoot me just to make a gunfighter name for themselves. I was forced into killing a man—just a kid, really—down in Mexico because he wanted to be the man who killed Coy Bell. I'm going by the name of John Denny now, but it's just a matter of time until I'm found out again. I have to keep moving and running. I don't want to kill again, and I don't want to run. It's a livin' hell—but I don't want to die either. I especially don't want to die as a woman killer, but I guess that's what will happen someday, somewhere."

Laurel May and Pete Jewel sat in the yellow lantern light in stunned silence. Silent minute after silent minute passed by. The cow in the cowshed bawled to be milked, and an owl hooted from the upper branches of the tree beside the pond.

At long last Coy rose and said, "Well, John Denny has got to get back to the herd. Somehow or another he's in charge, and it's his responsibility to get it and all the cowboys safely to the Black Hills."

When no reply came, Coy put his hat on his head and walked outside, his spurs faintly jingling with each step, his horse snorting softly with arched neck as he reached down to untie the hobbles.

"Coy . . . don't leave," Laurel May said from the doorway of the house.

"I've got to get back to the herd, Sunshine . . . Besides, it got pretty uncomfortable in there, didn't it. Things have happened that can't be undone, and there's no use trying."

"Please, Coy," Laurel May said, stepping outside to stand in the soft light of the rising moon, "don't leave yet. We need to talk alone. Walk to the barn with me . . . Please . . . So much has happened. We may never see each other again."

Coy tied the hobbles back around his horse's forelegs, and they walked slowly and silently to the barn. Laurel May lit a small lantern and from a pile of loose hay gathered up an armful and threw it over the fence to the cow. Then she leaned on the fence and asked, "Is this our fault, Coy?"

"You don't know how many times I've asked myself that, Sunshine. If I hadn't gone to New Mexico looking for you, Katy Hill and Walter would be alive—at least Walter would. I'm not sure what they had planned for Katy after they'd gotten your father's ranch, cattle, and money.

"Or if Walter and J.D. had told me that you weren't dead, I'd have left and gone to find you. I wasn't so noble that I'd have stayed to be sure they didn't steal everything your father had worked for. If I'd only *known* that you were alive—"

"And if *I* hadn't left like I did, *none* of it would have happened," Laurel May said.

"Why *did* you leave, Laurel May? When? And where did you go? How did you wind up here in Nebraska on a starve-out piece of farmland of all places?"

"I left when we stopped for the night outside Clarendon, Texas," Laurel May said. "When I told Walter I couldn't be his wife anymore, he slapped me and forced himself on me. I tried to talk to Daddy about it, but he couldn't understand what I was upset about. He said I ought to be giving him grandsons instead of complaining about an affectionate husband. I felt like Walter's whore and Daddy's breeding stock!

"I had four hundred dollars Walter didn't know about, hidden away. I told Jewel I was leaving and asked him to look after Daddy, but he insisted on coming with me. We just walked away after everyone else was asleep. I paid a man with a wagon fifty dollars to take us to Mobeetie. From there we caught a ride on a supply wagon to Dodge City. There we both worked in a café for a few months. The man we worked for has a brother in Sidney just a few miles east of here. I found out that he had this homestead that he had lived on until he got title to it but had moved to town to go into business and was wanting somebody to farm the place on shares . . . So, here we are—sharecroppers.

"I feel terribly guilty about what has happened. If *only* I had stayed. Other women have put up all of their lives with what I was having to endure. I was content to live with Walter like he was until . . ."

"Until when, Sunshine?" Coy asked.

"Until you came along and made me realize how empty my life was . . . Is that what started all of this, Coy? Did *we* sin so terribly that it has brought all of this about?"

"That's a question I've asked myself a thousand times. We didn't plan on feeling like we did about each other— and I couldn't stop myself from loving you. But if we hadn't, this might not have happened. On the other hand, Walter and J.D. were capable of anything it took to get what they wanted. Do you know that they had made arrangements for Katy Hill to be available to them on a moment's notice, and had done so weeks *before* you left Decatur?"

Laurel May took a deep breath. "My God! What were they planning?"

Coy shrugged. "Let's just say I was accusing them of something they might not have done, but were capable of doing—maybe even planned on doing sometime *if* you had not left.

"We'll never know all the whys in life, Sunshine. All we can ever know for sure is what *has* happened and what *is* happening right now. You were married and I fell in love with you. It nearly killed me to have to leave you in Decatur. I tried running from your memory, but couldn't. I tried drowning it in liquor, but that didn't work either. I tried saloon girls and whores to get you out of my mind, but that failed like everything else had done. At last, I decided to go back to Decatur and see you one more time. I didn't know why I was going or what I was going to say.

I wasn't going to try to take you away from Walter. When I got there you had moved and I was given the letter you left for me. It made me worry about you, and that's when I went to find you in New Mexico . . . If that's all wrong, then the devil can have my soul.

"Now, I guess I'd better get back to that herd. Like I said, we can't undo what's been done. I don't blame you for a thing, and I hope you can understand why I did what I did."

"Don't leave, Coy," Laurel May said softly as she moved to stand close in front of him. "Don't leave me alone tonight." The soft, longing, parted lips offered themselves to Coy as they had done in the cornfield. This time Coy and Laurel May kissed passionately. They were warm, wet lips. Her breath was sweet. His longing for her boiled.

He leaned over and kissed her throat. She closed her eyes and let him.

"If I stay," he said, looking deeply into her blue eyes, "you know what will happen."

"I know," she said. "I know nothing will happen that I don't want to . . ."

# CHAPTER 16

There was a refreshing coolness in the night air. Frogs were croaking in the pond. Laurel May smelled the delicious mixture of clean, dry hay and damp air. The barn was softly illumined by the full moon sinking now toward the western horizon. It was that quietest and most peaceful time of the day—the very earliest hours of the morning—when yesterday's troubles are but memories and those of today are out of sight somewhere beyond the sunrise.

Laurel May rolled onto her stomach and watched Coy dressing. "Did you sleep?"

"Better than I have in two years," he said.

She smiled. "I slept like a kitten. Who needs a bed when you've got a soft pile of hay to sleep on—and to make love on . . . What are you laughing at?"

"Quite a step down," Coy said as he buckled on his gunbelt, "from the feather mattress you had in your castle in Decatur, wouldn't you say, to a sod barn and a pile of hay?"

"I wish you wouldn't go," she said.

"I've got to take the herd on to the Black Hills, Sunshine—I've given my word. Besides, I'll get a bonus if we deliver on time, and that's money we need. I should be back within ten days. That'll give you and Jewel time to wind up your business and get packed."

"Then we'll go to Canada like you promised?"

"That ranch in New Mexico is rightfully yours, Sunshine—"

"It means nothing to me, Coy—only you do. Let J.D.

have it, and let God handle his punishment in His own way."

Coy nodded his agreement. There was a chance—a slim chance—he could clear his name if he went back with the real Laurel May. There was also a chance Laurel May could get the ranch if they went back. But there was also a chance he could hang and Laurel May could be killed— J.D. had proven himself capable of anything to get and hold his "empire."

In Canada they could maybe start a new life together with new names. There were cow outfits there that he should be able to work for, and maybe they could even start a little ranch of their own someday.

"We'll start out with nothing in Canada, Sunshine," Coy warned. "A pile of hay for a bed may be the most I can offer you . . ."

"Coy," Laurel May said, looking up at him, "I've been the queen of a castle and everything that goes with it, remember? I'd much rather be a cowboy's wife sleeping on a pile of hay—as long *you're* my cowboy and sharing the hay with me."

"You drive a hard bargain, lady," Coy joked, "but I think I'll just come back and take you up on it." Then he kissed her tenderly and stepped away from her embrace. "See you in about ten days," he said.

"Good-bye . . . Be careful . . . And, Coy, if anything should happen I want you to know that in spite of the mistakes we've made, in spite of things happening that both of us wish hadn't, I want you to know that I respect you and admire you and love you."

"Sunshine, I never thought I'd see you again, much less hold you in my arms and sleep with you on a pile of hay . . . Life is hard to understand sometimes, isn't it?"

"Impossible, Coy . . . Good-bye . . . Please come back to me."

\*　　\*　　\*

The next several days on the trail were uneventful. Each day dragged by painfully slowly for Coy as John Denny. It seemed to him the steers moved slower and slower each day. The nights in his bedroll or pulling his turn on night guard around the herd dragged by even more slowly. For the first time in two years he now looked forward to the future.

In spite of Coy's belief that each and every steer in the herd was traveling purposely slowly for no other reason than to aggravate him, the fact was they arrived at the appointed delivery point—the junction of Hat Creek and the Cheyenne River—one day ahead of schedule.

Coy watched with anxiety as a wagon approached from the east the morning after the herd's arrival. Two men who he knew would be in the wagon would be B.M. Bradley, the Texas rancher who owned the steers, and the Indian agent, a man named Stu Silverman. Besides them, there were two other men in the wagon.

Coy wished he could appoint some other cowboy to do the greeting and handshaking and smiling that would have to be done once the wagon rumbled to a stop, so he could remain unseen and unheard in the background. But that would not be possible, so he pulled his hat down—as all cowboys do when expecting the unexpected—sat on his horse a hundred yards east of the grazing steers, and waited for the wagon.

When the wagon stopped and people began disembarking, Coy walked his horse up to them and stepped off.

"You John Denny?" an old man with bushy eyebrows, a rough countenance, and western hat asked.

"I am," Coy said as he stepped forward and extended his hand. "You must be B.M. Bradley."

"How'd you know?" Bradley asked as he shook Coy's hand with a firm grip.

"Salt Roberts told me your name before he had to leave the herd, and out of this bunch you're about the only one whose legs look like they ever spent much time hangin' around a horse's belly."

From Bradley's smile it was obvious he took Coy's words as a compliment. "John," he said, "this is Benny Maxwell, my nephew." Coy shook hands with the man, small and slender, in his mid-twenties, and wearing wire-rimmed glasses, a bowler hat, and tie. "Benny's a Pinkerton detective from Denver."

Coy dropped the young man's hand and looked at Bradley. "What's goin' on?" he asked.

Bradley laughed. "Don't worry, John. Nothin's wrong. Benny just happened to be in the area, so I invited him to ride out with us."

Another man stepped up then—a forty-odd-year-old bareheaded man with windblown hair. "John Denny, this is Stu Silverman, the government agent who'll be receiving the cattle. How many did you get here with?"

"Fourteen hundred and ninety six. I got the ears off three that a twister killed in Nebraska a few days ago, and there was one that we just never found after the storm," Coy said as he reached out to shake the agent's limp hand. Just then someone said, "Look this way!" When Coy turned and looked, with his hand still clasping the hand of the agent, a camera popped, flashed, and smoked; his horse snorted and wheeled and it was all Coy could do to keep hold of the reins.

"Put that damn thing away!" Coy said.

Stu Silverman laughed and said, "That's Harvey Stroud, an official government photographer. He'll be taking pictures that will someday be in the national archives, Mister Denny. He might make you a famous cowboy—John Denny, the rugged Westerner who guided a large herd of cows across the arid western plains to—"

"And he might be wearin' that camera, too," Coy said as he stepped back into his saddle. "These horses don't savvy that kind of rig. You take all the pictures you want, Mr. Stroud . . . but you do it from a distance!"

"Well," Harvey Stroud said as they watched Coy trotting back toward the herd, "there's a novelty for you—a cowboy who doesn't want his picture made!"

"What do you mean?" asked Benny Maxwell.

"About the only two things that seem to attract most cowboys more than a camera are cheap whiskey and loose women," Harvey Stroud said as he removed a heavy photographic plate from his camera. "But I got his picture whether he wanted me to or not."

Of all the damn things, Coy thought as he trotted toward the herd—a Pinkerton detective and a camera! He had the urge to just trot on past the herd until he was over the hill and out of sight and then put his horse into a hard run back toward Nebraska and Laurel May. But that would be like sticking a red flag up and saying, "Look here, I'm really Coy Bell, wanted for murder—and no telling what all else by now. Catch me if you can!" And he wouldn't get the back wages he had coming or the bonus due him if he did that either.

He pulled his horse to a stop and thought for a minute. He looked at the two stub fingers on his left hand. Then, acting quickly, he pulled a pair of leather gloves out of a pocket on his chaps, pulled the gloves on, trotted back to the men standing around the wagon and said, "What do we need to do with the cattle, Mister Bradley?"

Bradley looked at Silverman. "You call it, Stu," he said.

"First, I need to look through them," Silverman said, "to look for any cull animals. Then you'll need to string the herd out and let it pass by me so I can get an accurate count."

"You want me to catch you a horse out of the remuda to ride?" Coy asked.

"I didn't bring a saddle," Silverman said, "so I'll just

drive through them in the wagon and point out the ones I want taken out."

"You'll play hell, too," said Coy. "You get in that herd with that rattlin' wagon and there won't be enough Sioux warriors on this whole reservation to hold 'em together."

"He's right," Bradley said. "Maybe we ought to just count 'em. We can figure two percent as culls at the discounted price stated in the contract."

"No," Silverman said. "It's not that I don't trust you, Mister Bradley. It's just not a proper way for me to carry out my business obligations."

"We've got an extra saddle in the bed wagon," Coy said.

"Put it on a horse then," B.M. Bradley said. "We sure don't want it to look like Mister Silverman's not fulfillin' his business obligations."

In a few minutes Coy came back, leading a little line-backed dun wearing an empty saddle. He handed the reins to Silverman and said, "This horse has got a lot of cow in him and he's pretty gentle but . . ."

"I'm sure he's quite adequate, Mister Denny," Stu Silverman said as he wedged a broad-toed shoe into a stirrup, grabbed the saddle horn in one hand and the cantle of the saddle in the other, and pulled himself up with two feet of slack in the reins.

The dun's eyes got big as he cocked an ear and snorted. Coy looked down at Bradley, who smiled quickly and shrugged.

"Will I need spurs on this animal?" Silverman asked.

"I kinda doubt it," Coy said. "If he doesn't go fast enough for you, just whip his ass with the ends of those bridle reins."

"You sure you don't want to just figure two percent as culls?" Bradley asked the agent. "That would be thirty head."

Silverman looked down and smiled. "What's the matter,

B.M.? You're not trying to pass off a herd that's ten or twenty percent culls to the government, are you?"

"I'll bet you there's not one percent," Bradley said. "But you go ahead and look."

Silverman rode into the herd and quickly found a lump-jawed steer, which walked quietly out. In a few more minutes he found a crippled steer and cut him out with no more trouble than he had had with the first one.

Then he found a brindle, high-headed steer with an abscess on his thigh where another steer had horned him.

This steer was wild and in no mood to be separated from the herd. The first time Silverman got him to the edge of the herd he threw his head up and darted past the agent and the dun horse and crowded in among the other steers.

"I think you're goin' to have to warm up ol' Dunny's ass," a nearby cowboy said to Silverman.

Silverman did just that—he brought the ends of the bridle reins down hard across each side of the dun's rump.

"I bet he'll work now," the cowboy said.

It took several minutes for Silverman to get the brindle steer with the abscess to the edge of the herd again. This time the dun horse was stepping more lightly and his ears were flicking back and forth.

The steer tried to run past them to the left, but the dun jumped in front of him. Instantly, the steer stopped and went to the left in a hard run. The little dun stopped, planted his hind feet, came around quickly on his left hock, then jumped over three feet until he was again in front of the steer.

The horse had moved so quickly to the left that one of Silverman's shoes slipped out of its stirrup. The agent reached for the saddle horn and tried to find the stirrup with the toe of his shoe. But now the steer came back even faster the other way, and even faster did the dun plant, roll, and jump again, this time to the right—while Silverman's body was still in motion to the left.

Now the steer made a run almost directly at the dun, at which move the dun sucked back so hard that Silverman, now with both shoes trying to find stirrups, was thrown forward until he had no recourse but to wrap his arms around the slim dun neck underneath him.

The dun, not thoroughly familiar with having a government agent hanging around his neck, squealed and tried to paw over his head with his forefeet. Then his head went down as he jumped backward, and Stu Silverman went as far in front of the horse as the bridle reins would allow him before turning a flip in the air and landing in the dusty ground on his back.

"You got ol' Dunny workin' now," a cowboy said as he rode up to the agent lying on the ground. "I seen a one-eyed steer over there you'll probably want to cut out. Here's your horse."

"Thanks," Silverman said with a grimace as he picked himself up and accepted the bridle reins from the cowboy.

"That was cruel of Mister Denny, B.M.," Benny Maxwell said as they sat in the shade of the wagon from atop a small rise of ground and watched the goings-on in the herd.

"Hell, Benny," the old cattleman said with a snicker, "that little dun is probably the gentlest horse in the remuda. Besides, nobody held a gun on that dumb son of a bitch and made him get on. You can't fault John Denny for that."

"Did you notice his expression when you told him I was a Pinkerton detective?"

"A lot of cowboys aren't in love with Pinkertons, son. Don't take it personal, but that includes me too."

"And what about the way he acted when Mister Stroud took his picture?"

"And nearly ran his goddamn horse off doin' it! I'd

have told Stroud the same thing. I just met John Denny, even though he's been on my payroll for over two months, but he's a cowboy, I can damn sure see that. He got that herd through in good shape and right on time with only one head unaccounted for. I can't fault the man for a damn thing."

"Uncle B.M.," Benny said, removing his glasses to wipe them clean, "I'm trained in the field of criminology. I know how the criminal element acts and reacts. I know how to look for small details other people would never notice—things like suddenly slipping on a pair of gloves."

"Good God, son!" Bradley declared. "And I know how to look for things that make a man that they never taught you in school. Things like the way he grips your hand and looks you in the eye, and sits a horse and handles men and cattle too, by God!"

"Now look down yonder," the old cowman said with a chuckle. "Silverman's suddenly decided there ain't near as many culls as he thought there was. He's cut out five head and he's quittin' because that little dun put some shit in his neck. I offered him a thirty-head cut and he turned it down. Each cull comes at a five-dollar discount to the government. That means he just cost his outfit a hundred and twenty-five dollars—which I'll get and which will pay John Denny's wages for two-and-a-half months, which is just about how long they were on the trail!

"I'll guarantee you, son, John Denny wouldn't have quit until the last cull had been worked out, no matter how many times he got his head stuck in the dirt."

"Okay, Uncle B.M., don't lecture me. I'm not a little boy, and I don't want to argue with you. I'm just saying there is something peculiar about the man that people without my training would never notice."

"And I'm just sayin' bullshit!" B.M. Bradley said as he walked off.

# CHAPTER 17

B.M. Bradley's herd of Texas steers was finally and officially handed over to a small band of mounted Pine Ridge Sioux not long before sundown. For the first time in nearly three months the cowboys had no night guard to stand. Nor was there any reason now to catch a night horse before dark. Thus the cowboys were relaxing around the wagon as darkness fell on the land of the Sioux, taking all the time they wanted to eat, smoke, tell tales, and rib one another. The only thing pressing in their minds was the fact that early the next morning Mr. Bradley was to come to camp and pay them off. Then they would have money to spend and time in which to spend it.

But one cowboy was not among the rest. John Denny was stretched out on his blankets beyond the circle of the campfire's flickering light, staring up at the stars. Nearby, his own little bay was hobbled and ready to go at a moment's notice.

Amid the banter and the laughter of the cowboys Coy heard something that made him sit up quickly—the rumble of a wagon traveling across the prairie.

"Good evening, boys," Coy heard B.M. Bradley say. "Where's John at?"

"Out there in the dark like an old coyote," a cowboy replied.

Coy quickly rolled his blankets, tied them on his saddle, and unhobbled the bay.

When he saw Bradley's slightly stooped form silhouetted against the camp fire and saw that he was alone he said, "Over here, Mister Bradley."

The old cowman talked in hushed tones but wasted no time and spared no words. "You're runnin' from something, aren't you, son?"

Coy's muscles bunched and his hand dropped toward the butt of the Colt on his hip. He didn't answer.

"That's what I figured—you got sense enough to keep your mouth shut, but we're too much out of the same cloth for you to lie to me. I respect that.

"That damned smart-aleck nephew of mine thinks a man has to go to school to know how to spot a man on the dodge. Hell, I seen it in you when we first talked this mornin'—seen it in your eyes, just like I seen it in my own several years ago. But what my nephew doesn't know is that you don't judge a man by his past—you judge him as you see him right then. You're a good cowboy, John, and you done me a good job. You helped me out of a hell of a pickle by being there to take over the herd and bring it on through when Salt Roberts come down sick.

"I figured I owed it to you to let you know that Benny and Stu Silverman have gone into Custer City to visit the Law and use the telegraph—by the way, that photographer got a damn good picture of you, too . . . So, I thought I'd come out before they got back and give you your money.

"Here's a hundred and eighty-eight dollars for your wages and a two-hundred-dollar bonus for gettin' the herd here and in such good shape." Bradley handed a small roll of bills to him. "And here's a little something else that I thought you might need—"

"Thanks for the offer, Mister Bradley, but I'll just take what I earned."

"Somehow I figured that's what you'd say. Good luck to you, son," Bradley said as they shook hands.

"Thanks for the warnin', Mister Bradley. I hate to leave without saying good-bye to the men. I wonder if you'd tell them for me in the morning . . . and tell them not to believe everything they hear about me. I killed a man all right . . . but that's all."

Coy Bell headed south in the darkness, toward Nebraska and Laurel May, with money in his pocket and a tightness in his chest, thinking about what would have happened without B.M. Bradley's warning, wondering how long he could keep avoiding the near misses. But for now he cared to look no further into the future than two days—the time it would take for the bay to carry him back to blue eyes and blonde, sweet-smelling hair.

Coy pulled up a mile north of the old farm midafternoon on a hot and sultry day. Then, like a coyote, he circled around to the east and came in from the south, stopping again under the tree beside the pond and letting the bay water while his eyes stayed on the sod house, waiting for Laurel May to come running out the open door to meet him. It was a fantasy he had had many times—him coming on horseback, hot and tired from a long day in the sun, to be greeted by Sunshine's smiling face, a prairie breeze gently blowing her hair.

He pulled the bay's head up. "Better slow down on that water, Blake," he said.

Then movement at the door of the house caught his eye . . . But it wasn't Laurel May running out of it—it was the milk cow sauntering out of it!

Coy slipped his Winchester out of its saddle boot, eased the bay to the house, stepped off, and peeked inside. The house was empty, and it was obvious the milk cow had spent considerable time inside.

Coy stepped back outside. "Sunshine!" he yelled. "Pete Jewel!" His heart beat rapidly.

Long strides carried him to the barn. He stepped through the door and into the part where he and Laurel May had slept together on the hay. The Winchester was cocked and the barrel leveled waist-high. Stepping from the bright sun outside it was hard to see.

"Mistuh Coy . . ." The voice was the barest of whispers.

"Jewel?" Coy yelled

"Over heah, Mistuh Coy . . . in the stall."

Coy found Jewel in the first stall, propped up against the milking stanchion. His head was swelled terribly and caked with flies and dried blood.

Coy lowered the Winchester and knelt slowly in front of him, as men do when kneeling before death. "My God, Jewel," he said softly, "what happened? Where's Laurel May?"

Jewel coughed feebly. "You got to listen quick, Mistuh Coy . . . and gets closer."

Coy put his face a foot from Jewel's, and that's when he saw that underneath the dark, dried blood and flies on the top of Jewel's head—he had been scalped.

"I's been holdin' on to my breath so's I could tell you . . . he took her . . . he took Miss Laurel . . . I couldn't stop 'im, Mistuh Coy."

"Who, Jewel? Who took her? Who did this to you?"

"A giant, big as the devil hisself . . . I tried to stop him from takin' her . . . . Will you bury me, Mistuh Coy . . out yonder 'neath the tree by the pond?"

"Sure, Jewel," Coy whispered. "How long ago did this happen?"

"Can't say . . . one day, maybe longer." Jewel coughed and closed his eyes and whispered so low Coy could not hear.

"Say it again, Jewel," he said as he put his ear next to the old man's swollen lips.

"J.D . . ."

"J.D. Davis?" Coy asked.

"The devil's workin' for him, Mistuh Coy . . . Said how surprised J.D. was gonna be. He put Miss Laurel on Sara an' said he couldn't wait to see J.D.'s eyes in a few days . . .

Miss Laurel, she said she didn't need no man but she need one now, Mistuh Coy . . . she need you . . . Where you been?"

Then Pete Jewel stiffened, twitched, and died against the milking stanchion.

Coy buried Jewel underneath the tree beside the little pond of water. Standing beside the mound of dirt he removed his hat and tried to find the right words to say. No words would come.

He sank to the ground on his knees with bowed head. So much killing and dying and brutality. "Thy will be done?" he shouted at the top of his lungs. "Is *this* Thy will?"

For the first time, Coy Bell felt inadequate, defeated. He blinked hard to hold back the tears he felt welling deep in his soul and pressing toward his eyes.

Then he saw the Winchester laying on the ground beside him and heard again Pete Jewel's dying words: "She need you, Mistuh Coy."

And in his mind he could see Laurel May as she must have looked as the man forced her on Sara the mule and left Pete Jewel behind freshly scalped.

Then Coy Bell picked up the rifle and looked at it. "If not Thy will, Lord . . . or mine . . . then the Winchester's."

# PART V

## GIVING THE DEVIL
## HIS DUE

# CHAPTER 18

Just as Coy was reining the bay around to start his long ride to New Mexico a horse carrying B.M. Bradley's nephew, Benny Maxwell, came around the corner of the barn.

Benny was carrying a rifle across the front of his saddle and quickly brought it up to point at Coy. "Hold it right there, Denny—or should I call you Coy Bell?"

"Call me anything you want," Coy said as he rode up to the young man, shed of his tie but still in shoes and bowler hat.

"So you don't deny it, huh? Well, it's just as well. I know all about you, and I'm taking you to Sidney and turning you in to the sheriff there."

"You did a good job of findin' me, son."

"Training in criminology includes field study in the art of tracking fugitives," Benny boasted.

"Well, I'm real proud for you," Coy said. "'You come alone, did you?"

"I'm alone at the moment, but there're law enforcement officers all over three states looking for you. So it would behoove you to come peaceful. Now remove your weapons carefully and drop them to the ground."

"Son, I got lots of ground to cover," Coy said as he reined the bay around.

"That was hardly a request, Bell," Maxwell said.

Coy spurred the bay into a trot.

"Bell! I have this weapon aimed at your spine! I demand you to stop!"

Coy kept the bay in a southbound trot.

A shot rang out and a bullet tore through the brim of Coy's hat. "That's mighty poor shootin' for a feller with all your training, Benny."

Benny Maxwell looked at Coy's trotting-off back over the rifle barrel in disbelief before lowering the rifle and trotting up behind him.

"Sir," Maxwell called to him emphatically, "you just as well should know that I'm prepared to follow you wherever you go—to the far corners of the earth even."

"Then you just as well come up here and ride beside me for a while so we won't have to holler at each other."

When Benny Maxwell came alongside him, Coy said, "Sort of like bein' married, ain't it? I mean, you bein' willing to follow me to the ends of the earth and all."

"This is hardly as funny as you seem to think it is, Bell. You're wanted for at least two capital offenses, you know."

"You're after the reward money, huh?"

"Pinkertons aren't bounty hunters, sir. The reason I'm taking you in is because I found out by wire that the company has a contract with a Mr. J.D. Davis in New Mexico whereby he agreed to pay two thousand dollars for ascertaining your whereabouts and bringing about your arrest."

"Good ol' J.D., huh? He's tryin' to deal himself a pat hand, looks like. You better go for the reward money, son," Coy said. "By the way, you ride like a sack of feed. Put more weight in your stirrups and get off your butt. Where in the hell were you raised anyway?"

"Philadelphia."

"It figures . . . Now that you've *ascertained* my whereabouts, what's your next move?"

"I'll stay right with you, keeping you under surveillance at all times, until I can inform the authorities."

"Well, Benny, I'm in as deep as a feller can get—I've got nothin' to lose, because they can't hang a man but once. I'm goin' to kill J.D. Davis and the feller that's takin' Laurel May Davis to him," Coy said with little emotion.

"But . . . that makes no sense! Laurel May Davis is already dead . . . you're wanted for her murder. Do you want to explain how—"

"No, I don't," Coy said. "I'm tired of talkin'. I just want to ride awhile."

And they rode well into the night, until Coy thought the bay could go no farther and still be able to cover forty or fifty miles the next day.

Coy found a little stream of water to make camp by, and had taken his saddle off, rubbed the bay's back dry with grass, and was already lying on his blankets when Benny Maxwell came dragging in.

"Kind of hard to keep me under proper surveillance when you're a mile behind, ain't it, son?" Coy asked as Benny stepped from his saddle.

Benny did not answer, but instead walked wobbly-legged to the stream to get a drink and wash the sweat and dust from his face. After spending a few minutes collapsed beside the stream he said, "What about a fire?"

"For what?" Coy asked. "You cold?"

"Hardly," Maxwell answered. "For coffee and—"

"You got any?"

"No."

"I don't either."

"What about food?" Benny asked.

"Be nice," said Coy. "You got some?"

"No, but surely—"

"Me neither. Chew on your latigo and go to sleep—unless you gotta keep me under surveillance all night. We'll eat tomorrow . . . and get in a *real* day's ride."

After a couple of minutes of silence Benny said, "You know I can't stand by and let you shoot anybody else."

"Don't see how you can stop me," Coy said. "But if you get in my way, son, I'll hurt you. Don't want to on account of your uncle B.M., but I will—you just remember that."

"You talk about it all so casually—doesn't life have any value to you?"

"Only one life has any value to me anymore, Benny."

"Yours I suppose."

"No . . . I realized just before you caught up with me this afternoon that my days are getting shorter and shorter. People are closing in on me from all sides. I don't have any hope of gettin' out of this alive. The only life that means anything to me now is Sunshine's, and for her to stay alive I've got to kill two men before I die—and anybody else who gets in my way."

"But you seem so lighthearted about it at times—"

Coy laughed. "One thing you'd better learn about men who see that their fate is sealed, son, is not to judge how they are feelin' inside by the way they are acting on the outside. You see, I'm in hell right now."

"Your conscience is tormenting you over the heinous crimes you've committed?"

"No," Coy said. "Did you ever fall in love with the most beautiful woman you ever saw? Did you ever lie with her in the moonlight and fall asleep together in a heaven you never knew existed . . . Did you ever do that, Benny?"

"I—I can't truthfully say that I have, sir."

"Then you can't know the hell that follows when it's taken away from you. Hell may be fire and brimstone and weeping and gnashing of teeth, but it all takes place deep inside where only you can see it and feel it. Hell is not being allowed the heaven that you know exists. It's knowing heaven is out there, almost within reach, but because of mistakes you've made you'll never touch it again."

Benny Maxwell lifted his head slightly and under heavy eyelids looked toward the "criminal element" lying silent now on his blankets. A coyote howled in the far distance and the prairie moon rising above the hills on the far side of the creek was shining off the metallic receiver of the Winchester that Coy Bell cradled in his arms.

# CHAPTER 19

"Why are you saddling up in the middle of the night?" Benny Maxwell asked as he sat up.

"It's not the middle of the night," Coy replied as he pulled his latigo snug. "The moon's almost down, the stars in the east are starting to dim, and it's time I was rattlin' my hocks toward New Mexico."

"So you can kill?"

'So I can save a life, if I'm not too late," Coy said as he slipped the Winchester into its saddle boot and then mounted the bay.

"I'm following you, you know?"

"Not unless you get astraddle that sorrel of yours, you're not," Coy said as he rode away.

Just before noon, out on the open plains of eastern Colorado, they spotted buzzards circling high in the air a mile ahead. Coy and Benny approached a carcass.

"It's Sara, the mule he had Laurel May on," Coy said as they looked down at the dead animal, swelled in bloat. "Looks like she's been here about two days."

"Her throat's been cut," Maxwell said.

"You're hell for pickin' out details, Benny."

"But who cut it and why?"

"The man who's got Laurel May did it because the mule played out on them. That means he'll have to put Laurel May on behind his horse until he can steal another one—which he probably has done by now. But it slowed him down for a little while at least."

'But *how* can he have Laurel May Davis when—"

"When I've already killed her? The truth is I didn't kill

Laurel May—or the woman posing as Laurel May. J.D. knows it and that's why he's hired someone to take Laurel May to Redondo, New Mexico."

"And you mean to catch up with them before they get to Redondo?"

"Well, that would be sweet, but not very likely. I just hope to travel enough faster than they do to get to Redondo about the same time they do."

"But how do I know he's even got a woman with him—much less that she could somehow be Laurel May Davis? And what would motivate him to cut the mule's throat?"

"The same thing that motivated him to scalp a harmless old man and leave him for dead—some men just have an itch to kill things."

"Like you, you mean?"

Coy looked at him through eyes squinted in the bright sunlight. "I got no itch for it at all, Benny. I hate to kill. Got no stomach for it. If I could, I'd melt these guns of mine down into fishin' weights and spend the next forty years up in the mountains beside some pretty lake full of trout and watch the beaver play and the elk come out to water early in the morning. But it's too late for that—maybe it always was too late for me . . . Come on, Blake," he said to the bay underneath him, "we're burnin' daylight."

Two hours later Coy stepped off and tightened his cinches. When he got back in the saddle he looked behind him as he took down his rope. Way back, just a dark speck on the prairie, was Benny Maxwell. Coy shook his head and built a loop in his rope. Then he shifted his gaze toward the cattle grazing in a sage-covered draw a half mile ahead.

When Benny finally dragged to the bottom of the draw, he found Coy lying in the grass, eating beef roasted over a sage-wood fire. The partially skinned carcass of an Angus yearling heifer was nearby.

"Want some lunch?" Coy asked.

Benny's eyes got big as he beheld the juicy steak on a stick dripping tallow into the coals over which it was suspended.

"Isn't that illegal?"

"I wouldn't be at all surprised."

"I can't eat any of that without permission from the animal's rightful owner."

Coy shrugged. "There's an old cowboy sayin': 'No game, plenty of beef—what the hell, let's eat' . . . Write me up in your surveillance report if it'll make you feel better."

Benny hesitated only a few seconds, only long enough to look up and down the draw, before climbing down and taking a piece of meat off the stick. When the Pinkerton sat down with the steak in his hands and began tearing hungrily into it with his teeth, Coy looked at him over his own steak and grinned.

The next day at midafternoon Coy and Benny topped a rise of ground in the southeastern plains of Colorado to a see a wagon sitting in the middle of a narrow road in the draw below them.

Coy pulled his bay to a stop, looking hard at the wagon.

"It's just an abandoned old wagon," Benny said.

Coy looked at the young Pinkerton but said nothing. Then he rode off the rise of ground in the direction of the wagon.

"Why . . . Look, Mister Bell . . . It looks like there's some people sleeping beside that wagon."

Coy looked at him again without speaking.

"I wonder where their horse is and why they—"

"He took their horse," Coy said as they trotted closer to the wagon.

"He? . . . You mean the man you are following? You think . . . Oh, my God!" Benny Maxwell said as he reined up his sorrel. "My God!"

"We'd better see about 'em." Coy said.

"Good Lord!" Benny exclaimed, just before he turned his head away from the man and woman lying on the ground beside the wagon. "What . . . Why? . . ."

"Looks like the man's throat's been cut," Coy said as he stepped to the ground. "But the woman's alive. Get off your horse and unsaddle him, Benny."

"But why . . ."

"Goddammit, son, just do what I say!"

While Benny unsaddled his sorrel, Coy leaned over the woman. She was perhaps fifty years old. It appeared she had been struck in the face a few times, and her dress was badly torn. Her underclothes had been removed.

"She might make it if we get her to a doctor in time," Coy said. "Hitch your horse to the wagon. You'll have to just go down this road until you find a town, or some homestead or ranch—there's probably one within a few miles." As Coy talked he gently lifted the woman from the ground and laid her in the bed of the wagon.

"You'll have to help me load the man's body, Benny."

Benny Maxwell gasped. "I don't think I can, sir, I—"

Coy grabbed his shirtfront in one hand and slapped him hard across the face with the other. "Goddammit, son, you'll do what you've got to do! This isn't school anymore, this is the real thing—this is real life and death out here. It's hard and ugly as hell, but sometimes life is like that. Now, help me!"

Pale and shaking, Benny did as he was told. When the man's body was in the wagon Coy said, "Now get up there on that wagon seat and take off."

"Sir," Benny said, almost apologetically, "you should know that when I get to a town I'll be obligated to tell them about you and that you're headed to Redondo to kill some men."

"Benny," Coy said as he stepped into the saddle again, "you do anything you feel you have to do—just like I will . . . Now get the hell out of here!" With that Coy quickly took his rope down and hit the sorrel across the butt with it.

"I'll be coming to Redondo as soon as I can, sir!" Maxwell said as the wagon careened down the narrow road.

# CHAPTER 20

Buffalo was a full six-foot-four with a shaggy mane, dirty and streaked with gray. A wide nose, pale eyes, and forehead were the only flesh exposed on his bearded face. He spoke rarely, but constantly wallowed a huge plug of tobacco from one side of his mouth to the other. A steady ooze of that tobacco kept his mouth and chin whiskers glistening with a brown glaze. He was wide-bodied and drop-bellied. A huge hairy hand constantly scratched, rubbed, and fondled that belly.

No one, even those who knew him best, knew where he came from or what his real name was. He was more animal than human, not only in appearance but in character as well, knowing nothing of the emotions that separate humans from the other members of the animal kingdom . . . such as remorse or love.

Buffalo was a self-promoter who dealt in human misery and profited by other people's mistakes and misfortunes. Whether it was selling whiskey or guns to the Indians and collecting their scalps for a dollar apiece, or whether it was tracking down army deserters for forty dollars a head, his livelihood was earned at the expense—and pain—of others. But he was good at what he did, and now, as he sat Indian fashion on the ground in front of a small fire looking at Laurel May, he was filled with sadistic pride. Tomorrow he would look into J.D. Davis's face and tell him how good the hunting—and his tracking—had been.

Laurel May sat on the ground with her feet pulled up underneath her, her hands tied in front and her head down. Her long blonde hair was filthy and matted, her face red from sunburn and smudged with dirt, her neck brown with dirt except for the white streaks where sweat had run. Her dress was no less dirty, and it was snagged and torn.

Buffalo had made camp in the bottom of a ravine in which the southwest wind swirled loose sand into eye and nose. It was past sundown but not fully dark. Laurel May was not aware that Buffalo had come to stand in front of her until she felt his hands on her shoulders.

She immediately tightened with fear as those huge and dirty hands pushed her back onto the ground and lifted her skirt. "No . . . no," she muttered feebly, unable to offer any other resistance.

Just after sundown the next afternoon J.D. Davis answered a knock on his door.

"Hello, J.D.," Buffalo said. "Huntin' season's over."

The look on J.D. Davis's face told of his surprise. He stepped back and let Buffalo enter, then took a quick look outside before closing the door. "What are you doing here?" he asked.

"What'n the goddamn hell do you think I'm doin' here? You hired me to do a job, didn't you?" Buffalo grinned, showing tobacco-stained teeth. "Job's done."

"You mean you—?"

"Found our game in Nebraska."

"In Nebraska! Which one?"

"The girl with the yellow hair. She was with the old nigger."

"Laurel May and Jewel," J.D. Davis said rather slowly, as if he were having trouble believing what Buffalo was telling him. "What . . . did you . . . do with them?"

Buffalo spat tobacco juice on the parlor floor. "Let's talk money," he said. "Ten thousand cash."

Davis laughed lightly. "Our deal was for four thousand, and I've already sent you a thousand. That leaves three thousand—but I've got to have some kind of proof. You were supposed to get in touch with me once you had her located. You weren't fool enough to think I'd just hand over three thousand dollars without having some kind of proof, were you?"

Buffalo sat down on the sofa and looked around the expensively furnished room. Then he opened a leather pouch tied to his thick waist and tossed a stiff object covered with thick, kinky gray hair to J.D. Davis, who caught it and looked at it.

"Look familiar?" Buffalo asked.

"No . . . ," replied J.D. as he turned the object over and looked more closely at it. "What is it? Why should it look familiar?"

"It's the old man's top pelt," Buffalo said, and laughed as Davis dropped it to the floor and stepped back from it.

"Put ten thousand dollars in my hand right now," Buffalo went on, "and you can have one with long golden hair on it—I'll even let you take it off yourself."

J.D.'s head jerked up. "What in the hell do you mean?"

"I mean I packed the game you wanted to you, still on the hoof—almost in your backyard."

"You sadistic bastard!" exclaimed a visibly shaken J.D. Davis. Then, "You haven't brought her back here, have you? You damn fool idiot! What if somebody—"

"Nobody but you will—as long as I get the ten thousand dollars."

"You stupid fool!" exclaimed a red-faced J.D. Davis. "The last thing I wanted was for you to bring her here!"

"Just get me the ten thousand and you can stop your frettin', J.D.," Buffalo said with a shrug of heavy shoulders.

"Don't threaten me, Buffalo," warned J.D. "I didn't get where I am by letting nobodies like you make their own rules and tell me what to do. I'll pay you what our agreement called for and not one more penny, and then you'll leave and you'll never come back here again." Then J.D. Davis moved to a floor safe beside an oak desk in the corner of the parlor, where he spun the dial back and forth a time or two with a shaking hand. He opened the heavy door, withdrew a stack of bills, counted them out, and turned around with them in his hand, saying, "There's thirty-three hundred dollars here . . ."

Buffalo rose to his feet and walked to the door, throwing his head back and bellowing in laughter. When he reached the door he turned around and said, "When I come back you'll have the rest of the ten thousand and you know you will. Ten thousand is a pretty cheap bargain, considerin' what you're gettin'—your empire *and* your neck."

Buffalo lumbered to his horse and mounted.

"Wait—!" J.D. yelled as Buffalo wheeled his horse around and trotted off, still laughing.

When J.D. Davis closed the door and turned around, Maggie was standing over Pete Jewel's dried scalp where it lay on the floor. She was dressed in an ill-fitting drab gray dress. One thin hand was tightly clutching her gray uncombed hair at the base of her neck. The pale skin on her face seemed to be stretched too tightly for comfort over her skull. Her lips seemed practically nonexistent, her mouth but a bitter horizontal gash.

"I heard," she said in a weak but shrill and cracked voice.

"What'll we do, Maggie?" J.D. asked. "He's brought Laurel May back here and we don't have the money he's demanding for her."

"Get it from the bank first thing in the morning," she said.

"We don't have it in the bank. We are about broke. We only have a hundred head of cows left and the bank won't loan us more than a couple of thousand on them."

"You've squandered everything, you fool! If only your brother were still alive . . ."

"Well, goddammit, Walter's not alive!" J.D. yelled, and kicked the door so hard the window glass in it shattered. "He's dead and buried in the ground, and we will be too if Laurel May talks . . ."

Coy had pushed the bay relentlessly since he and Benny Maxwell had parted company. He could not have covered the hundreds of miles separating the homestead in Nebraska from Redondo Mesa any quicker. But now, as he watched a new day come to life, he had a sickening feeling that he should have pushed himself and the bay even harder, rode all night long every night instead of just the last one.

Hundreds of feet below him sprawled the headquarters of the ranch that legally and morally should now belong to Laurel May. Looking down upon the ranch headquarters, where lanterns were beginning to shine yellow through scattered windows, he tightly gripped his Winchester and thought about Sunshine, whose life he valued more than his own, and pleaded to God in silent, cowboy prayer that he was not too late.

# CHAPTER 21

Coy waited on the rim of Redondo Mesa as a slow and cold late-August rain began to fall. He donned his slicker and huddled between a large rimrock boulder and a wind-twisted rimrock cedar, continuing to wait and watch. J.D. emerged from the big rock house and walked to the barn. A few minutes later he rode out of the barn on a paint horse and headed north on the road that led to the town of Redondo.

Knowing the time for being cautious had long since passed, Coy mounted the bay and spurred him off the steep trail on the east side of the mesa that had carried him up several hours earlier. Once he leveled off on the plains below he reined toward the north and struck a long trot through scattered mesquites and cholla cactus. On the outskirts of Redondo he stopped and looked behind him to check his back trail. Then he pulled his slicker collar higher, his hat lower, and his Winchester out of its saddle scabbard.

After checking the rifle's chamber to be certain a live round was waiting patiently in front of the firing pin, he slipped the carbine under the long-tailed slicker and rode into the town of Redondo, where, for two long years, a hangman's noose had been patiently awaiting his return.

The rain was coming steadily down as Coy rode down the town's wide main street. Water was already collecting in puddles and filling up wagon-wheel ruts. The few saddle horses tied to railings along the street stood with heads down and drooping tails clamped tight. Among

133

those horses was but a single paint tied in front of the Rancher's and Merchant's State Bank of Redondo.

Coy dismounted on the opposite side of the street, loosely tied his bay to a railing in front of Smith's Mercantile, and waited on the covered boardwalk, leaning against a support post with his Winchester snug underneath his slicker, dry and ready.

Three doors down, barely noticed by Coy Bell, squatting on the boardwalk and leaning against a wall was another man watching the bank with equal silent intensity—a giant of a man, with shaggy hair and a heavy gray beard.

Half an hour later J.D. Davis stepped out of the bank and stood motionless for a few seconds underneath the overhang. Coy felt his heartbeat quicken, but only watched as J.D. Davis walked east down the boardwalk until he came to the open door of the Maverick Bar. When Davis disappeared into the bar Coy untied his bay, mounted, and rode to the railing immediately in front of the Maverick where he dismounted again, pulled his hat down further over his eyes, and stepped inside.

Standing at the bar at a point closest to the door, Coy ordered a shot of whiskey without lifting his eyes or looking at the bartender.

While downing the drink in a single gulp as inconspicuously as he could, Coy let his eyes sweep the around the bar until he spotted J.D. sitting in a corner alone with a bottle of whiskey on the table in front of him.

Then another man entered the bar and stopped just inside the threshold. Out of the corner of his eye Coy studied him, suddenly recognizing him as the same big man who had been squatting on the boardwalk a few doors down from where he had been watching the bank.

The man walked past Coy, sauntered across the bar, and pulled out a chair at the table where J.D. Davis was nursing the bottle of whiskey. The look in J.D.'s eyes confirmed for Coy who this man must be—and it hit him with a sudden, ferocious impact.

Coy felt cold sweat begin to pop out on his face. The hand holding the Winchester beneath his slicker tightened as his thumb came to rest on the heavy hammer. As he watched the two men lean toward each other and talk quietly, hatred seethed in his heart. He was sure he could kill both men before either could stand—J.D. first, then the other one.

But he subdued his own lust for blood and turned his eyes back toward his empty shot glass on the bar in front of him. Now was not the time—in spite of the rare opportunity provided him. Not until he knew what they had done with his Sunshine.

"Hey, mister!" the bartender said.

Coy's thumb brought the hammer underneath it instinctively to full cock as he lifted his head.

"How many times do I have to ask you—do you want another drink?"

Coy looked at him and shook his head as thunder rolled outside. Suddenly now he was nervous. He was scared—not so much of dying, as of failing.

Suddenly Benny Maxwell walked into the Maverick Bar.

"I was told I might find J.D. Davis in here," the young man said, shaking the rain from his hat and looking around the bar.

Coy turned his head, hoping to avoid being recognized by Benny.

"Coy Bell!" Maxwell exclaimed.

Chairs scooted across a hardwood floor and hands reached for Colts as Coy's Winchester came up from underneath his yellow slicker.

A barmaid screamed and Benny Maxwell yelled, "Don't!" But the calling of Coy Bell's name had ignited a short fuse on an explosive combination of raw nerves and cordite.

"You—!" J.D. Davis exclaimed as his whiskey-slowed hand brought his revolver up.

Coy tucked the butt of the Winchester underneath his arm as his trigger finger released the firing pin. The rifle roared and belched out a short stab of flame, rolling gunsmoke, and 200 grains of soft lead. The bullet hit J.D. in the heart and knocked him backward, wide-eyed and twitching, into a darkened corner of the bar.

Buffalo swung around in a snarling crouch, his .45 at full cock, while Coy was still levering a new round into the Winchester's firing chamber.

Benny Maxwell hurled himself into Coy, and they both tumbled to the floor as Buffalo's slug shattered the window above them.

Sheriff Joe Talbert burst through the door firing one barrel of his shotgun into the ceiling and yelling, "Hold it!"

Talbert's attention was on the big man across the room with his Colt ready to fire, so Coy was able to come up on his knees with the agility of a cat and swing the Winchester like a club, striking the sheriff in the stomach.

As Talbert doubled over, the second barrel of the shotgun discharged, shattering the mirror behind the bar and adding to the smoke-filled chaos in a barroom gone mad.

Buffalo dashed for the door with an animal-like growl, running into the bent-over Talbert like a charging bull and sending him rolling out the door, across the boardwalk, and facedown into the muddy street beyond.

Quickly out the door, Coy stepped into the rain as Buffalo slapped the butt of his horse with the bridle reins and left in a hard run through the mud. Coy brought the Winchester hard against his shooting shoulder and took deliberate aim on the broad back. But the Winchester remained silent.

Although he knew he could have severed Buffalo's spine, he stayed the shot and lowered the rifle. As he turned to get his bay he saw Sheriff Talbert had risen to his hands and knees in the mud.

He stepped behind the sheriff, placed a boot on his rump and shoved, sending the lawman face down into the mud once again.

Once Coy was in his saddle Benny Maxwell appeared wide-eyed and pale on the boardwalk in front of him. Benny's small, double-action .38 was in his hand, but the hand hung loosely at his side.

"That big man is the one who had Laurel May," Coy said. "He was making a deal with J.D. Now J.D.'s dead. You made me kill him before it was time. That means Buffalo's deal is dead, too . . . and Laurel May along with it, unless I can get to her in time. She's not worth anything to him now, but he can't let her go."

People were fast gathering and pointing. Coy reined the bay around in the direction Buffalo had fled and told Benny, "You get in my way again before I'm finished and I'll kill you without blinking an eye. After Talbert there gets out of the mud, you can tell him the same thing."

# CHAPTER 22

As Coy Bell rode in a long lope out of Redondo he knew he was on his last ride. He had a posse on his trail again, or soon would have. But this time the Silent Trapper of the Black Woods—as an old Indian friend of Coy's referred to Death—had a bait that Coy could not circle and ride away from.

He looked back toward the town of Redondo. It had stopped raining, but a mist almost obscured the town, which was only three-quarters of a mile away. Between himself and Redondo, coming fast through the mist was a lone horseman. Coy had slipped the Winchester back into its boot once he had cleared town, but now he reached down for it again. Was Sheriff Talbert coming after him alone, without a posse? That didn't seem likely, and it should take the posse at least another fifteen minutes to get underway.

Coy drew out the Winchester and waited as the figure came nearer. A posse he would have run from, but one man held no fear for him now. He had no desire to shoot the rider, but he had even less desire to have him at his back.

As the rider drew nearer in the mist, Coy recognized him by the way he rode—or rather flopped around in the saddle. It was Benny Maxwell, and Coy decided not to wait for him.

Coy put the bay in a short lope. He could no longer see Buffalo ahead of him, but he could read his tracks easily in the mud.

Finally Benny Maxwell caught up, his horse lathered and nearly spent. "You'd better go back, Benny," Coy said.

"Mister Bell," Benny said, "I'm so sorry about what happened in town . . . I didn't know . . . I shouldn't have . . . Things happened so fast I'm still not sure about any of it—except that you killed J.D. Davis."

"Go back," Coy said.

"That was the first shootout I've ever witnessed. Why didn't you kill the other one when you had the chance?"

"Because he's the only one who knows where Laurel May is. If she's still alive he's got her hidden somewhere where she may never be found—not alive anyway."

"How will you find her?"

"Follow him . . . and hope."

"But the posse . . ."

"Yeah . . . the posse," Coy said. "That means I don't have much time."

"You could wait and tell them about it all. Don't you think Sheriff Talbert will—"

"I'm wanted for the murders of Walter and Laurel May Davis . . . and now I guess J.D. Davis too. Talbert will have his hands full keeping the posse from lynching me as soon as they get their hands on me—he may even help them."

"I'm going with you," Benny Maxwell announced.

"For what?"

"To help you find her—Laurel May Davis."

"All of a sudden you believe me, huh? Go back, Benny. I don't need or want your help. You'd just get yourself killed—maybe by me."

"If you kill this man and find Laurel May, will you give yourself up then?" Benny asked.

"What for?" replied Coy. "So they can hang me from the nearest tree? Or even worse—so I can sit in a jail cell and watch them build my gallows?"

"What other choice do you have? If we can find Laurel

May in time and get somebody from Decatur to identify her, a jury will surely not . . ."

"Damn! You are a dreamer, son! Maybe you ought to be writing some of those yellow-backed dime novels they're sellin' back East about us Westerners. How would you make this one end? . . . I save Laurel May from the villain, the sheriff all at once sees how innocent I am, the people of Redondo throw a big party for Laurel May and me, and then we live happily ever after at the ranch that was stolen from her? Is that sort of how you've got it worked out in your mind, Benny?"

"But couldn't it—"

Coy pulled the bay to a stop. "Goddammit, Benny! *Can't you see* that this is the real world you're in the middle of now! Here, dreams—and men—both die . . . and they die goddamn hard, too!" With that, Coy put the bay into a lope again, down the muddy road.

Again, Benny Maxwell caught up with him. "I—I'm going with you," he said. "I followed you from South Dakota to Nebraska and rode with you most of the way from Nebraska to here. Somehow, I know I'm involved in this and I've got to see it to the end—with you. You'll have to shoot me to stop me."

"If you get in my way, Benny, I'll do just that. If you stay with me, I'll use you any way I can. The killin's not over with yet. You'll be ridin' with an outlaw who's wanted dead or alive."

Following Buffalo's tracks was easy for two miles after Coy Bell and Benny Maxwell joined forces. But then the tracks turned west off the road just after entering the Davis/VanHughes Ranch property and disappeared as they crossed a flat covered with cholla cactus and tall tabosa grass.

"We've got to get up high," Coy said, "where we can see a lot of country."

They found a trail going up the northwest slope of Redondo Mesa, but before reaching the top they had climbed above the low-hanging clouds and could see nothing below.

Coy pulled to a stop on the trail. "Won't do us any good to go any higher," he said.

"What'll we do now?" Benny Maxwell asked.

Coy shook his head. "I'm afraid—"

"Did you hear that?" Benny asked.

"No . . . what?"

"I know I heard a horse nicker—back in that direction." Benny pointed down and toward the west. "Do you think it's the posse?"

Coy reined his horse around and started him down the steep slope they had just been climbing. "The posse will probably stay together—they feel safer that way—and horses in a bunch won't usually nicker. More like a horse by himself feelin' lonesome—or one horse greeting another . . . You're sure of what you heard?"

"I'm sure, Coy," Benny said with a nod. "I heard a horse nicker from somewhere down there." Again he pointed down and to the west.

As they lay on stomachs on the narrow spine of a ridge that ran perpendicular to the mesa before disappearing into it, Coy whispered to his young companion, "I'm sure glad I insisted on you coming with me, Benny. And I'm sure glad you heard that horse nicker while we were up on the side of the mesa."

They saw Buffalo hurriedly breaking the camp he had made amid a heavy growth of cedars that hugged the bottom of the slope. The horse he had come in on was still saddled and hobbled, and now he was throwing a saddle on another horse.

"Where do you think she is, Coy?" Benny Maxwell whispered.

"I'm afraid to think, son . . . That dirty son of a bitch

might've—" Then Coy's words broke off short as his very breath stopped.

"There she is, Coy!" Benny exclaimed in a loud whisper as Buffalo disappeared into the cedars and then came out with a woman behind him whose hands were obviously tied in front of her. "My God, Mister Bell, look at that—he's got a rope around her neck and he's leading her like she was a horse!"

"Must be four hundred yards down there," Coy said, more to himself than to Benny Maxwell. "If it was half that distance, I'd take a chance on dropping the bastard in his tracks, but it's too risky from here."

"What'll we do?"

"When he leaves he'll stay close to the bottom of the mesa and work around its west side, then he'll head south. We've got to swing around in front of him and pick out a good place where he'll be passing."

Coy mounted the bay at the bottom of the ridge. Benny Maxwell mounted his own horse, then sat twisting and squirming in the saddle as he watched Coy begin an arching ride that would take him around and finally in front of Buffalo and the woman.

Benny felt very alone and scared, and suddenly longed for the safety of the posse that he knew could not be far away. He no longer felt at all like a Pinkerton detective. Instead, he felt like a schoolboy who had no business being involved in any of this. But there was something about Coy Bell—and his resolve—that he could not help but admire.

He looked again at Coy Bell, who had struck a long trot and was already on the verge of disappearing in the mist. Then he struck the rump of the horse underneath him hard with his bridle reins and loped toward the outlaw, relieved, and scared, by his final decision.

He knew now for sure that the man they had followed all the way from Nebraska did indeed have a woman with him, obviously against her will. The fact that she could possibly be Laurel May Davis, however, still seemed too incredible for Benny to believe. He didn't know who the woman was that Coy was so bent on rescuing, but he was convinced that in Coy's mind, she was indeed Laurel May Davis.

Benny did know one thing for sure, however—the man who held the woman, regardless of who she was, was capable of the most horrible and senseless violence imaginable. He had seen that firsthand when he and Coy came upon the couple beside the horseless wagon in Colorado.

Coy and Benny rode hard in a wide arch in a determined effort to get in front of Buffalo. They kept to the low places as they rode, draws and dry washes. Their horses were forced to either jump or dodge untold clusters of prickly pear, cholla cactus, and beargrass. Coy rode with the ease and grace of a man born to the saddle, but Benny hung on for dear life.

They rode until they were able to swing south, putting the mesa about a mile east of them. After riding another mile or so south they began to angle toward the mesa again, soon coming upon scattered cedar trees that grew thicker the closer to the foot of the mesa they got. When they were two hundred yards from the talus escarpment of the mesa and on the southern slope of a small rise, Coy pulled to a stop, shucked off his slicker, handed Benny the reins of his bay, and told him to stay with the horses while he bellied up to the top of the ridge to look. No sooner had he peeked over the top than he withdrew from the crest and came back to the horses in a run.

"We're just right," Coy announced. "The bastard will be passing right by here in a few minutes." He withdrew his Winchester from its scabbard and threw it to Benny. Coy removed his gunbelt and Colt revolver and hung them on his saddle horn. He instructed Benny to hand him his small double-action .38 caliber Smith and Wesson, which

he placed in the middle of his back in the waistband of his
Levi's.

They were in an open, grassy area but no more than
twenty yards east of an area heavily timbered with big
cedars.

"I'll be sittin' here in the open when he tops that rise,"
Coy said. "You get back in those cedars with the rifle and
wait. I'll lure him on down close to palaver some way.
When I reach up and touch my hat with my left hand you
shoot."

Benny broke out in a sudden, cold sweat. "You mean . . .
Mister Bell," he said in a shaky voice, "you surely don't
expect me to shoot the man in cold blood?"

"It would be nice if you could," Coy said in a calm voice,
"but I don't trust you shooting that close to Laurel May.
He's got her on the horse behind him. But you have to
shoot, Benny—shoot over his head, or shoot your foot, or
shoot anywhere you want to, I don't care—but, goddammit, when I touch my hat with my left hand you'd better
shoot somewhere 'cause that's when I'm reaching for your
little .38, and I'm dependin' on you to distract him enough
to give me an edge."

"But—"

"But, nothin'!" Coy said. "Now they'll be toppin' that rise
any time. Get your ass in those cedars and shoot that
goddamn rifle when I touch my hat!"

"But what if—what if you get shot?"

"Simple," Coy said with a grin. "If I go down, then it'll
just be you and him. You'll have a good chance to kill him
with that rifle, provided your nerves hold out. Now, get on
over there in those cedars . . . and good luck to you."

# CHAPTER 23

Benny sat on his horse in the cedars, no more than a hundred feet from Coy.

Coy yelled, *"You there!"* in a very loud voice when Buffalo and Laurel May topped the rise and were clearly within Coy's view.

*"Let's talk,"* he continued. Then he lifted his gunbelt off the saddle horn, held it out to his side for a few seconds, and let it fall to the ground. *"With J.D. dead, the woman is not worth anything to you, but she is to me. I want to talk trade with you."*

There was silence. Buffalo and Laurel May stopped six feet in front of Coy. The rope that Buffalo had led her out of the cedars with earlier was still around her neck.

"What was J.D. going to pay you for her?" Coy asked as he rested his hands nonmenacingly on top of his saddle horn.

"Enough," Buffalo said in a deep, gravelly voice.

"But J.D.'s dead now, so she's no good to you anymore," Coy said.

"She gives me pleasure," Buffalo said in a vile manner, "anytime I want it. She's better than a dirty squaw and cheaper than a whore . . . I think I'll keep her for a while yet."

Coy's jaw muscles tightened and his face turned red. Benny thought that was when Coy would reach up and touch his hat with his left hand, signalling him to shoot. But Coy didn't make his move, which puzzled Benny.

"I'm Coy Bell," Coy said, "and I'm worth a lot of money to the Law."

"That's no reason for me to let the woman go," Buffalo

said. "I can just shoot you and haul your carcass in for the reward."

"It won't be that easy," Coy said, "on account of that man in the cedars there with the rifle aimed at you."

Benny cocked his rifle, and all hell broke loose.

Buffalo heard the hammer clicking back and swung his rifle toward the cedars that only partially concealed Benny. At the same time Coy's right hand went behind his back for the .38.

Benny squeezed the trigger on the rifle, aiming at least two feet above Buffalo's head.

Coy fired. The horse Buffalo and the woman were on fell out from under them and they both went sprawling on the ground. The horse Buffalo was leading snorted and set back, broke his lead rope, and ran off. Coy's horse snorted, too, and tried to wheel away both from the shooting and from the horse that had just collapsed so suddenly in front of him.

Coy shot again from his wheeling and rearing horse. His gun this time pointed down where Buffalo was on his knees with the rifle in his hands pointed up at Coy.

Benny saw Buffalo flinch and he knew Coy's bullet had struck him somewhere. But instead of going down he took dead aim at Coy.

Trembling uncontrollably, Benny levered another shell into the rifle's chamber, put Buffalo's wide chest in the sight of his rifle, and squeezed the trigger.

Benny's shot came only a split second before Coy's third shot. Both rounds hit Buffalo again, Benny's in the chest and Coy's in the head. This time Buffalo went down like a rag doll and lay without twitching.

Buffalo lay dead with his blank eyes staring up at the blue sky. The horse he and Laurel May had been on was dead, too. Laurel May lay motionless, facedown on the ground.

Coy jumped down from his horse and ran to Laurel May. He gently rolled her over. She was bruised and skinned up, but she was alive and breathing and her eyes were darting about in fear.

Coy buried his head in her neck and cried. Then he lifted his head and wiped dirt from her face with a gentle hand and whispered, "Oh, my Sunshine . . . Sunshine . . ."

But her lips did not move and only fear showed in her blue eyes. Coy continued to stroke her face with his fingertips and he kissed her softly on the mouth, but she gave no indication that she was aware of anything.

There was a commotion from the top of the same rise that Buffalo had ridden over only a few minutes earlier. It was the posse, made up of at least twenty riders, poised on the hilltop above them—trying to understand what they were seeing.

Then the posse fanned out and started off the hill in a collective long trot, rifles drawn, some resting across the fronts of saddles, others up and at the ready.

"Coy Bell!" It was Sheriff Talbert's voice. "Your runnin's over. You're goin' in one way or the other."

Coy stood up with the woman in his arms as he watched the approaching posse come off the hill and fan out wider and wider.

"Take care of her, Benny," he said as he kissed her again gently on her lips and handed her to Benny. "Will you promise me? You're the only person in the world I can trust."

"But—"

"Promise me, Benny! Promise me!"

"I'll take care of her, Coy . . . But what are you going to do?"

"The only thing left to do," he said as he picked up his rifle from where Benny had laid it on the ground and then gestured toward the coming posse with his head.

"No," Benny said, "Talbert's a fair man. You'll get a trial and—"

"And I'll get hung . . . I'd rather end it this way, Benny.

Everybody who knows what really happened is dead now, there's no one left to tell the truth, except for Maggie—and she never will. Laurel May can't stand up to testifying and I could never put her through it anyway. Besides, who'll believe that she is really Laurel May Davis after all this time."

"I believe it, Coy,'" Benny said.

"Thanks, Benny," he said. "And thanks for comin' with me. There's not a man anywhere that I'd rather ride with. That's why I know you'll take care of Laurel May."

"But she needs you . . ."

Coy shook his head. "It was never meant to be. What happened between us was wrong and has brought nothing but death and heartache. Just look around you, Benny. I'm damn tired of it all, too. Laurel May is still young enough to start over . . . but not me. When a man crosses a certain point there's no going back—I crossed that point a long time ago."

"Coy Bell!" It was Talbert again. "Lay down your weapon and walk toward us with your hands high in the air!"

Coy began walking toward them, but the rifle stayed in his hands.

"Drop the rifle, Bell!" Talbert instructed. "Don't be a fool!"

The posse members who did not already have their rifle butts hard against their shooting shoulders now put them there.

Coy was not going to stop, nor was he going to put his rifle down. Benny had come to know him well enough to know that. Coy was determined neither to run anymore nor to hang. But Benny had great faith in the Law's ability to sift through all the facts and come up with the truth.

Benny laid Laurel May down in the grass, grabbed Buffalo's rifle off the ground, and rushed toward Coy from behind and struck him hard. Coy's knees buckled and he fell facedown in the grass. Within moments an unconscious Coy Bell was surrounded by Talbert and his posse.

# PART VI

## THE WAGES
## OF SIN

# CHAPTER 24

When Coy regained consciousness he found himself tightly bound with his hands behind his back. He did not say a word to anyone, but when he looked at Benny his eyes showed a combination of resentment and resignation.

"We'll have to bring a wagon out from town for the woman," Benny said to Talbert. "There's no way she can ride."

"Who is she?" Talbert asked, along with a hundred other questions.

"I firmly believe," Benny stated, "that she is Laurel May Davis."

"Impossible," Talbert answered.

Benny recounted the story Coy Bell had told him, about Walter Davis and the phony Laurel May, about J.D.'s hiring Buffalo to kidnap the real Laurel May . . .

Benny Maxwell was hailed a hero for bringing in one of the most wanted men in the Southwest. He arranged to have the $2,500 reward money on Coy's head used for the care of Laurel May, as it was apparent that she would require much care and attention for some time.

News swept the countryside quickly that Coy Bell had been captured and was awaiting trial in Redondo. Coy was arraigned and officially charged with the double murders of Laurel May and Walter Davis. No charges were filed against him for killing J.D. as there were plenty of witnesses to the fact that J.D. had drawn his gun first.

In a surprise move it was announced that Benny Max-

151

well, the Pinkerton who brought Bell in, would now defend him in court.

A trial date was set for the nineteenth of September, which allowed Benny three weeks to prepare Coy's defense. At first Benny received no cooperation from Coy, who would only ask how Laurel May was. Benny told him she had changed little, if any, from the way she had been when Coy first rolled her over in the grass out there at the foot of Redondo Mesa. She ate very little and had not spoken a word. Most of the time she wore only a blank stare on her face, but at times her eyes would dart around here and there and she seemed to be afraid. She could not respond to people, even when Benny mentioned Coy's name.

Dr. Blackmore said he thought she would snap out of her condition soon, but how soon he could not say. He thought it not a good idea to take her to see Coy in her present state, as the sight of him might trigger more unpleasant memories and force her mind to withdraw even further. He wanted to keep her in his home and away from everybody.

Since Laurel May was in no condition to testify, Benny sent a wire to the sheriff of Decatur, Texas, a Dan Leathers, asking if he knew of anyone who had known Laurel May well enough while she lived there to identify her beyond a shadow of a doubt. Leathers expressed shock at the thought that she might still be alive and said that both he and the Methodist minister, a Reverend Stroud, were making arrangements to travel to Redondo and would be there to identify her at the trial.

Benny believed the trial would definitely go in Coy's favor if Laurel May Davis herself could take the stand and tell the same story as Coy, and if two very well-etablished, prominent, and credible witnesses would testify that she was indeed Laurel May Davis, daughter of Leonard VanHughes and wife of Walter Davis. Once her identity was established, the rest of the defense should be no problem and it would be apparent that someone else had killed the lady posing as Laurel May—and who else were there but Walter and J.D. Davis, *the* two people who *had* to know she was a fraud? Their co-conspirator, Maggie, had run off shortly after J.D.'s death. Her flight did not exactly prove Coy's story was true, but Benny expected that her disappearance would at least raise doubts.

A week passed, then two weeks. There was still no change in Laurel May, and Benny began to fear she would not be able to testify. When her condition still had not improved three days before the trial was to begin, he went to the judge, David Witherspoon, and asked for a postponement. After a quick conference with Dr. Blackmore, Witherspoon denied the motion for postponement on the grounds that Dr. Blackmore could not say for sure when, if ever, the young woman would be able to testify.

Things were certainly not looking good for Coy's case, but still there was Sheriff Leathers and Reverend Stroud coming from Decatur to establish the fact that whoever the woman buried in the town cemetery beside Leonard VanHughes was, it was certainly not Laurel May Davis.

A jury was picked, Coy was led into the courtroom under heavy guard and in chains, and the trial began. There was not a vacant seat in the courtroom. Every square inch of standing space along the walls was occupied and people clustered outside and tiptoed and strained neck and ear in order to see or hear anything going on inside. Boys climbed over the newly constructed and waiting gallows and held mock hangings of Coy Bell. Reporters from many large newspapers, not only in the West but from back East as well, were on hand interviewing everybody who had a story to tell either about Coy Bell or the Davis family.

The prosecution presented its case first. Sheriff Joe Talbert testified about being led out to the Davis/Van-

Hughes Ranch by Coy two years earlier and how he had been told then by both Laurel May Davis and Maggie the housekeeper that Coy had attacked Laurel May in Decatur in 1888. He also told about being called out to the Davis/VanHughes Ranch the night Laurel May Davis was killed, how he had been told by Walter and J.D. Davis that Coy Bell had kidnapped her, and of the terrible disfiguration of Mrs. Davis's face, how it had been caved in by a rock after she had been shot with a shotgun. This caused women in the courtroom to gasp and cry and men to lean heads together and whisper with determined head nods.

When Benny cross-examined the sheriff he asked whether, in Talbert's opinion, the shotgun blast alone was a serious enough wound to kill the woman.

"Certainly was—no doubt about it," the sheriff answered.

"Then why would you think it necessary that her face be smashed in with a rock, also?" Benny asked.

"You'll have to ask him, I guess," Talbert replied, pointing toward Coy.

"One more thing, Sheriff . . . when you viewed the dead woman"—he always avoided calling her Laurel May or Mrs. Davis—"could you have told who she was if you had not already known . . . or was her face in such a sad state that that would have been impossible?"

"I suppose it would have been hard to tell who she was from her face alone . . . but it was Mrs. Davis, Maxwell, you just as well accept that."

"Or was it the woman you had been deceived into believing was Mrs. Davis, when in fact it was a saloon girl from Amarillo, Texas, named Katy Hill, who just happened to look somewhat like the real Laurel May Davis! And isn't it possible that Walter and J.D. Davis themselves killed her and smashed in her face so nobody *could* recognize her!"

Bryan Samson, the special prosecutor appointed by the

governor to handle the case, jumped up and shouted his objection to Benny's "outlandish supposition and theatrics."

The prosecution's main contention was that Coy Bell was simply a madman whose obsession for Laurel May Davis ultimately led him to destroy the entire Davis family. The prosecution rested their case.

As Benny's first witness for the defense, he called Coy himself to the stand.

"Do you, or have you ever known, a woman by the name of Laurel May Davis?" Benny asked.

'Yes," Coy replied. During the whole trial he never once ducked his head or answered in a weak voice. He looked everyone straight in the eye and answered straightforwardly in a firm voice.

"This is the same Laurel May Davis who was the daughter of Leonard VanHughes and the wife of Walter Davis?"

"Yes."

"When and where did you first meet her?" Benny asked.

"At the VanHughes Ranch west of Decatur, Texas, in May of '88."

"And what was your relationship with her?"

"I fell in love with her," Coy answered.

"And did you have any reason to believe that she had similar feelings for you?"

"She loved me, too."

"And what led you to believe this?"

"She told me."

"Did she commit adultery with you?" That put the courtroom in a buzz.

"No," Coy answered. "She wasn't capable of it. She felt too bound by her marriage vows to Walter."

"What happened between the two of you then—in 1888 at the ranch in Decatur?"

"She told me I had to leave . . . and I did."

"And have you seen Laurel May Davis since the spring of '88?"

"Yes . . . I ran into her on a sharecropper's farm in Nebraska a little over a month ago—her and old Pete Jewel."

"Were you surprised to find her?"

"Yes . . . I thought Walter had killed her."

"And why would you think that, Coy?"

"I went back to the ranch at Decatur two years ago and found they had moved . . . but Laurel May had left me a letter that said she was afraid of him." Coy pulled out the letter and handed it to Benny, who opened it and gave it to the judge. After the judge read the letter he handed it to Samson.

"I would like for the letter to be read to the jury, Your Honor," Benny said.

"I object, Your Honor!" Samson exclaimed. "There is no way the authenticity of this letter can be verified. Anybody could have written it!"

Judge Witherspoon thought a second and then said, "I agree. The letter will not be read to the jury."

Benny continued, "So anyway, Coy, when you found Laurel May in Nebraska you were very surprised—in a happy way?"

"In a very happy way," Coy said. "I had been convinced I'd never see her again, that she was lying buried somewhere in an unmarked grave."

"Very well," Benny said. "And did you find you still loved her when you saw her again?"

"More than ever," Coy said. "I was in charge of a herd of cattle going to the Sioux in the Dakotas and had to leave the next morning. When I came back, about ten days later, I found Pete Jewel dying and Laurel May gone."

"And have you seen her since?"

"Yes . . . three weeks ago when me and you killed the son of bitch who brought her here for J.D. Davis."

Bryan Samson, the prosecuting attorney, came to his feet. "I object, Your Honor! There is no proof that J.D. Davis had anything to do with that woman's being here—whoever she is!"

Judge Witherpsoon sustained the objection and told Coy to just answer the questions and not interject things he had no way of proving. Coy looked straight ahead without responding.

After things had settled down a bit, Benny asked, "Coy . . . did you kill Laurel May Davis?"

Coy looked at him with his steel blue eyes and said, "Of course not—she's still alive."

"Did you kill anyone you thought was impersonating her?"

"No . . . I could never kill a woman."

"What happened that night out at the Davis Ranch—the night you are accused of killing Laurel May?"

"The woman, Laurel May's imposter, got scared that Walter and J.D. would kill her to keep her quiet. I told her I'd help her get away if she'd tell me everything she knew. I met her a mile or so east of the house in the dark and put her on my horse behind me. We hadn't gotten very far when Walter and J.D. stopped us. I tried to make a break for it and Katy Hill—the woman I'd picked up—was shot. The same shot that killed her nearly killed me—that's how I lost these fingers—but I kept riding and got away."

"And did you come back two days later and kill Walter Davis?"

The courtroom got quiet. Coy looked at Benny a long time and then said, "Yes."

"Tell me about it." Benny said.

"I'd lost a lot of blood . . . there's a lot of it I don't remember. But somehow I got back to the ranch house and went in the barn. I heard men talking—it was Sheriff Talbert and the posse. Talbert was telling J.D. and Walter that they'd start looking for me after the weather warmed up and the snow melted. They were sure I was dead. That was when I knew I was getting blamed for killing Katy Hill.

"The posse left, and J.D. went to feed the horses. Me and Walter were in the barn alone. I stepped out where he could see me and I think I asked him what he had done with Laurel May . . . I remember him saying that everything that had happened was mine and Laurel May's fault. He started bringing a shotgun—or maybe it was a rifle—around. I yelled for him to stop—but he didn't. I guess then's when I killed him. All I really remember is some shooting and then me finding my bay and riding out into the cold and the dark."

It was then the prosecution's turn to examine Coy, and the first thing Samson asked was, "Would you say you were obsessed with Laurel May Davis, Mister Bell?"

"I loved her," Coy said. "Still do."

"You fell in love with her at the ranch in Decatur, Texas, is that right?"

"Yes."

"And when the Davises moved out here you followed them. Is that not right also?"

"I had to make sure Laurel May was okay," Coy said.

"Mister Bell," Samson said rather smugly, "were you at the Thanksgiving party thrown by the Davises at the new lumberyard two years ago."

"I guess you must know that I was," said Coy.

"Then you were there, were you not, when Walter and Laurel May got up in front of the crowd and Walter publicly thanked her for giving him the best years of his life—then gave her a necklace and she passionately kissed him? Did you see that, Mister Bell?"

"It wasn't Laurel May up there with him."

"Isn't it true that you couldn't stand to see how happy Laurel May was with her husband?"

"It wasn't Laurel May!" Coy repeated, louder than before.

"Maybe you learned she had had many men over the years and that you were just another on a long list of illicit lovers and you—"

Coy was out of his seat in a flash and, in spite of the chains slowing him down, he had his hands on Samson before two deputies could pull him off.

Samson smoothed out his coat and said, "I see you have a rather short and violent temper, Mister Bell. I only have three more questions for you: Do you admit to killing Laurel May Davis?"

"No—she's not dead," Coy said.

"Second—do you admit to killing Walter Davis?"

"Yes," Coy said.

"And do you now feel, or have you ever felt, Mister Bell, any remorse for the killing of Walter Davis?"

Coy looked straight at Samson. "The son of a bitch needed a killin' . . . If he was to come back to life today I'd do everything I could to kill him again."

Benny Maxwell slowly shook his head.

Samson said, in a very satisfied voice, "No further questions, Your Honor."

"I think we'd better recess until the morning," Judge Witherspoon said.

"Drinks are on me at the Maverick," someone yelled as the courtroom emptied.

# CHAPTER 25

The next morning, Benny Maxwell called Reverend Stroud and Sheriff Leathers from Decatur to identify the woman Dr. Blackmore brought into the courtroom as being none other than Laurel May Davis herself.

Benny called Reverend Stroud to the stand first. After he had been sworn in, Benny had him identify himself and explain to the jury his relationship with Laurel May Davis. He had been her minister for five years in Decatur. He even had married her and Walter.

Then Benny called Sheriff Leathers to the stand. As it turned out, he and Joe Talbert knew one another on a professional basis, so there was no question as to his actually being who he said he was or to his credibility. He stated that he had been elected to his first term of office not long after Walter and Laurel May were married and that he had come to know both of them on a first-name basis.

Benny had Stroud and Leathers stand together in front of the witness box while Dr. Blackmore brought Laurel May in.

The courtroom hushed and heads turned toward the door. When Dr. Blackmore stopped, with Laurel May standing beside him, just inside the doorway of the courtroom, people talked in hushed whispers or stared silently.

"Will you bring her on down the aisle, please, so the witnesses can have a good look at her," Benny said.

They stopped again in the aisle where the first row of spectators were seated.

That was the first time Coy had seen Laurel May since

the day at the foot of Redondo Mesa. Coy was taken aback by what he saw. Laurel May was wan and thin and she stared straight ahead without emotion.

With Benny's eyes on Laurel May, he said, "Now Reverend Stroud and Sheriff Leathers, have you ever seen this woman before?"

He expected an immediate answer, but it did not come. The courtroom grew still and very quiet.

Then Judge Witherspoon grew impatient. "Well, gentlemen?" he said.

"I'm not sure, Your Honor," Reverend Stroud said.

Coy jumped to his feet and Benny and he exclaimed at the same time, "What do you mean you're not sure?!"

Benny tried to collect himself and quietly told Coy to sit down.

"You mean," Judge Witherspoon said, "that you can't say for sure whether you have ever seen this woman before? You can't say whether she is or is not Laurel May Davis?"

"I thought I could, Judge," Sheriff Leathers said. "I thought I could tell in an instant one way or the other, but . . .'"

"But what?!" Witherspoon asked.

"But now it's hard to say for sure. It's been a couple of years and . . ."

"Laurel May was always smiling and laughing and had ribbons in her hair," Reverend Stroud said.

"And she wasn't anywhere near that thin," Sheriff Leathers said, "and those dark circles underneath her eyes . . ."

"And her hair was always long," Reverend Stroud said, "not bobbed off short like her's is."

"Her hair was so dirty and matted my wife had to cut it," Dr. Blackmore said, half apologetically.

"If we could talk to her," Reverend Stroud said. "I could ask her questions that no one but Laurel May would know the answers to. Being her minister for five years we exchanged many confidences."

"She hasn't said a word since I've been taking care of her," Blackmore said. "Nor has she ever given any indication that she has heard a single word said to her. Look at her now—she seems completely unaware that she's the center of attention here."

"I'm sorry, Your Honor," Reverend Stroud said. "There is a very good likelihood that she *is* Laurel May Davis—"

Bryan Samson was on his feet again. "That means there is also a likelihood that she is *not* Laurel May Davis. Isn't that right, Reverend?"

"We just cannot say for certain," Reverend Stroud said.

Bryan Samson sat down, wearing a wide grin.

Benny took of his glasses and shook his head. He had built his whole case around proving that Laurel May Davis was alive!

"Well, Mister Maxwell," Judge Witherspoon said, "are you through with these witnesses?"

Benny shrugged. "I guess I am, Your Honor."

"Mister Samson?" Witherspoon said.

"I have no questions for them, Your Honor," he said.

The courtroom began to stir to life again as Stroud and Leathers walked past Benny and took their reserved seats in the gallery.

"Is the defense ready to call its next witness?" Witherspoon asked.

Benny faced the judge and said, "The defense rests."

Bryan Samson and Benny Maxwell made their closing remarks to the jury.

"It has been proven," Samson said, "that Coy Bell *is* a violent man. He has *admitted* that he killed Walter Davis—a deed which *must not* go unpunished. We must not let one tragic event prohibit us from rendering swift and just punishment to the perpetrator of other tragic events. Gentlemen . . . do your duty."

"Gentlemen," Benny said as he stood before them with his glasses in hand, "what is Coy Bell's crime?"

Three hours later the jury announced that they had reached a verdict.

The jury foreman stood as a hush fell over the courtroom.

"What is the verdict you have reached, Mr. Foreman?" Judge Witherspoon asked.

"Your Honor, we find Coy Bell guilty.

"Will the defendant please rise and face the bench for sentencing. Before I pass sentence, Mister Bell, is there anything you wish to say?"

"No," Coy said.

"Very well. Coy Bell, you have been found guilty of the crime of murder by a jury of your peers. By the authority vested in me I hereby sentence you to be hanged by the neck until dead. The date of execution will be at sunrise on the tenth of October. May God have mercy on your soul."

# EPILOGUE

At sunrise, Coy Bell stoically climbed the gallows steps. He asked Sheriff Talbert that a hood not be placed over his head. Talbert stayed the hood. He had no last words on the gallows, except to request burial on some hilltop outside of town.

Coy Bell died at the end of a rope on October 10, 1894.

His punishment was unjust. If he was guilty of any crime, it was not murder. Sometimes justice must lie in God's own hands and not in the hands of His imperfect creatures.

"Take care of Sunshine," were his last words to Benny Maxwell who visited Coy the night before the hanging.

In time, Laurel May recovered—although she never did fully remember what all had happened after Buffalo found her and Pete Jewel in Nebraska.

Eventually, she moved away, married, and raised three children.

Laurel May never tried to prove who she was or to claim the ranch in New Mexico. She said she had to leave it all behind her and start over. But she never forgot Coy Bell, and she journeyed back to visit his lonely grave many times over the years.

If you have enjoyed this book and would like to receive details on other Walker Western titles, please write to:

Western Editor
Walker and Company
720 Fifth Avenue
New York, NY 10019